I0835658

The Lovers

Catherine Rey

the LOVERS

GAZEBO BOOKS – ELIZABETH BAY 2018

Gazebo Books
P.O. Box 375
Summer Hill
New South Wales 2130
Australia
gazebobooks.com.au

First published 2018

National Library of Australia
Cataloguing-in-Publication Entry
Rey, Catherine, 1956–
The Lovers
First edition
ISBN 978 0 9876191 1 2 (paperback)

Cover and interior design by Mountains Brown Press

Cover and frontispiece image: Rob McHaffie,
Touching face II 2014, oil on linen, 46 x 36 cm,
Kleimeyer Stuart Collection.
Courtesy of Darren Knight Gallery.

for Etienne, for Sophie

Act I

Ernest Renfield
Longland
New South Wales

Officer Lawson, pleased to meet you! Come inside! Come in! Goodness me, it's freezing outside. What an endless winter indeed. Let's go to the sitting-room. This way... to the right and then down the hall. Yes, it's a big place, far too big for me. When was it built? 1887. Further down the corridor... nearly there. Now this door to the right, please... After you... Have a seat. Would you fancy a drink? A tea? A coffee? A drop of alcohol maybe? No? Not even a glass of water?

Lucie, yes, Officer Lawson, have you heard anything yet? What happened to her, for God's sake? I'm completely wrecked... When was the last time we spoke to each other? Well, that would have been the Sunday before last... I had organised a dinner party to celebrate our anniversary, let's call it an engagement party. Lucie has been my common-law wife for two years and I intend to marry her.

You winced. I saw you. Yes, you winced, didn't you? I've never been married, that's right, I've never had lasting relationships, I've never had children and still I want to marry her. She's young enough to be my daughter, well, yes, that's what people say. I've never been bothered by what people think. Truly, I don't give a damn about what people think of me.

Yes, I had chosen the Sunday before last to celebrate Lucie, to honour her, to tell her she was my ladyship. I invited those friends who've always liked and supported my work. Gary Whitehall, my art dealer. Peter Brown, the art critic, who came along with his boyfriend Rony Hack, a young stage actor, not very talented but extremely good-looking. Pietro Negri, the Melbourne publisher. Edy Garudo, the architect, who flew in from Cairns. Garudo? You must've seen Garudo's fountains of glass in Canberra at the National Gallery... Magnificent, I agree... Samuel Hackton, the celebrated playwright, flew in from Canberra with his wife. My brother Raphaël came as well. As none of them were going back before the next day, they all stayed the night. I had a full house.

That's right, the Sunday of the party was the last time I saw and spoke to Lucie... Why didn't I immediately report that she was missing? Well, good heavens, I assumed she had just gone away for a couple of days. The business card of a local taxi driver was lying on her dressing table. I gathered she was off to her friend Nicole's. She was giving herself some breathing space before coming back. I didn't want to worry myself sick.

Had she ever gone off? No, never, but I wasn't at all surprised since we'd had a few words that morning... Yes, well, Lucie got cross with me. When she checked the guest list, she saw Rosy Barth's name and worked herself up into a jealous rage. Why? I had a fling with Rosy... That was ages ago. We were so young. Rosy was only eighteen. We hadn't seen each other in such a long time and I was looking forward to catching up. Rosy is an old girlfriend. Lucie had nothing to fear; yet my little missus got it all wrong. Look, Officer Lawson, it wasn't a serious fight, just a little argument.

I beg your pardon? What was she wearing when I last saw her? Hmm, a long black gown and high-heeled shoes... Oh yes, and a tweed jacket.

As for the last guests, they left my place at four-thirty, quarter to five, yes, it would have been at sunrise. The three couples that stayed went to bed. And after everyone had gone? Well, I went straight to bed myself. Lucie was nowhere to be seen. I called out to her, checked to see if she was in the bathroom. That's when I saw the business card of the taxi company on her dressing table. That's about it. I was exhausted. I fell asleep in no time.

Huh? Why didn't I call the police instead of

letting Nicole do it? Well, that's not exactly what happened. Let me explain, Officer Lawson. Nicole called me last Wednesday because she hadn't heard from Lucie. I was extremely surprised as I assumed Lucie must have been with her. Nicole thought we should call the police and I agreed. That was indeed the best thing to do. So I went to the local police station to file a report... Yes, I filed a report on Thursday morning at the Watooga police station and drove back shortly after to provide a recent photo of Lucie... Yes, absolutely, the report was filed on Thursday, four days after Lucie disappeared. You can check. Huh? You already have?

Was I worried? Yes and no. In all honesty, I thought Lucie needed some fresh air. Life with me can be stifling. Life with any artist can be stifling. Do you think Picasso was an easy fellow to be around? I can be difficult to live with, I must confess. Everyone will agree to that! People say I'm hard work. No argument there! When I'm engrossed in my painting I need peace, solitude... I cannot stand any disturbance. Besides, Lucie and I, we're a modern couple. Mm... How would I put it? We act like modern people do. I like my freedom and I don't abide by the "stultifying discipline of monogamy", as D.H. Lawrence put it, and the same goes for Lucie. I don't object to her going without warning wherever she wishes.

Has she ever been unfaithful to me? I don't think so, but as you may have gathered, I don't subscribe to conventional views. Lucie doesn't either. Faithful, unfaithful, it's a bit outdated, isn't it? If she wants to have fun, why can't she? Yes, we live like a modern couple. Still, she gets jealous, I know. Women can be irrational! You're married, aren't you, so you'll agree with me. Lucie was jealous of a woman she hadn't even seen, jealous of my past... But you've got to understand, living in Longland is an entirely different life for Lucie. She might have felt like a fish out of water. In all honesty, I don't know if she's enjoying living in Australia. I could fathom the workings of her mind when she moved here two years ago. She looked happy. Then her moods started to swing. I slowly lost track of her. She grew distant, cold, her behaviour became disconcerting. I worried for her. I was glad when she befriended Nicole, very glad... Yes, Nicole is French as well.

I began to wonder if I had done all that I could for her. Are you happy here, I would often ask. Would you like to move somewhere else? If the house isn't to your taste, well, let's sell it and move to a warmer place, by the ocean, in Queensland. Of course, this is a beautiful house, on ten acres of land, it's in a good location, not too far from

Sydney. I could get good money for it… Oh yes, I would happily move somewhere else, but I must admit, I'm used to Longland. I grew up in this house and after my parents' death, twelve years ago, decided to settle back here. Sydney is too noisy for me these days. Relocating at sixty-two doesn't thrill me. But I didn't want to be selfish. I would do whatever Lucie wanted, telling her, if you want to leave, we'll leave. If you don't like the house, I'll sell it. I'm convinced I did all I could for her.

Anyhow, the more I did the less happy she was. That was my impression. The harder I tried, the more she grew distant, irritable, neurotic. Women know how to string us along, don't they? The more we give, the more they want. They love us as long as we feel sorry for them. Now, I guess I sound cynical, I shouldn't, no, I shouldn't. That's not fair… Oh, look, I'm mad at her for taking off like a thief. My weakness is that I love being on my own and, by the same token, dread being on my own. That's the paradox. The truth is that I cannot conceive of my life without Lucie.

I was instantly besotted when I met her at the State Library. She was wearing a floral summer dress and gold sandals. Her toenails were painted red. These ten dots of bright red nail polish were fascinating… She was the prettiest little faun I'd ever seen. She stood in profile before the front desk and she instantly reminded me of this painting by Domenico Veneziano, *Portrait of a Young Lady...* I've seen it, at the Kaiser Friedrich Museum, in Berlin. Have you been there? You must go. What an ugly part of town, by the way. Between Friedrichstrasse and Alexanderplatz. I remember how stunned I was. I can still feel the tears running down my cheeks. Such an enticing painting and not a wrinkle after five hundred years! Imagine a young maiden in profile against a cobalt blue sky. Her flesh and her hair with the translucent tint of smooth ivory. She wears a brocade dress. Her plaits are tied up, twisted into the shape of a small peasant bonnet... Lucie reminded me of this painting. Her alabaster skin, her Venetian blond hair, her large grey eyes, her long delicate neck, her round shoulders, her grace, her divine breasts beneath that thin summer dress... What a beauty! I have a photo of her. Take a look! Isn't she stunning? When I saw her, I knew I'd been waiting for her my whole life. And when I heard her lilting accent as she spoke to the librarian, I felt like falling to my knees. I looked at her. She smiled. She smiled, yes! Women don't smile at me these days. I'm too old. Too fat. They only smile when they realise who I am... Renfield, the famous Ernest Renfield! But when that foreign beauty smiled at me, I walked up to her. She said her name was Lucie... Lucie, I thought, I'll carry you like a princess, like a queen, carry you so that your legs never tire and your toes never touch the ground. I'll carry you through life so that you never have to worry. I'll brush your hair at dusk before putting you to bed. I'll sing you lullabies. *Do, do, l'enfant do...* Yes, that day, I thought life was worth living again.

The photo? You'd like to keep this photo? Oh, not this one, it's my favourite photo, but let me search through my desk. I shot dozens of photos of her... By the look on your face, Officer, I can guess what's going through your mind. Oh yes, I can read minds. Ernest Renfield, the renowned painter, has been granted all a man could wish for. He's had his fill of women. What more does he want? What difference is a pretty girl going to make? Well, believe me, Lucie's made a hell of a difference.

Did you know that talent wears out? Life runs by. You have less energy. Strength fades away. And one day you wake up, you look in the mirror to realise old age has snuck up on you without your consent. Would you believe me if I told you that I've kept the shirt I was wearing when they took a photo of me for the cover of *Time* magazine? 1966. I was twenty-eight. Quite a while ago. I had a solo exhibition at the Museum of Modern Art, in New York. Two hours before the photo shoot, I ran to Madison Avenue to buy a new shirt. I wanted to look good. This would be my lucky shirt. It was the following morning that I realised my photo would make the cover of *Time*. On the day I bought the magazine, I couldn't help looking around to see if anyone recognised me. Did anyone recognise me? No! No one... How ironic, how funny! People hurried past me... And you know I haven't thrown away that flowery shirt, it's upstairs, somewhere in a drawer. Smells musty. I look at it every so often. I look at it, touch it, smell it, so that I remember who I was, what I've done, just to have the solid proof that New York wasn't a dream.

I'm turning sixty-three at the end of the year, not long to go. What choice do I have? Tell me, Officer Lawson. Do I have any choice? Truly, the answer is no. I have to keep painting. It's my life. I have nothing else. I've been given one unique talent, and I don't intend to bury it in the ground like that stupid fool did in the parable. A coin buried in the dirt will never bear fruit. Remember the Parable of the Talents? Aha, you aren't into parables. Well, the point of the story is that you've got to let your talent flourish, expand, burgeon, grow. Paint, paint and paint! That's the one lesson I got from the Good

Book. I like the Parables. They're intriguing. As for the rest of the Bible, it's rubbish. Anyhow, if I don't paint, I cannot stand the masquerade called life.

But let's get back to the point. I began going downhill. Recalling what I'd accomplished, the MOMA, the Tokyo exhibition, the Helsinki retrospective, the many distinctions; none of these achievements mattered anymore. No, they meant nothing! See, when I started painting at the age of eighteen, I saw that my generation was fed up with the old way of fashioning the world according to European dictates. Society took a radical turn in the Seventies. People loosened up. All over the world, things were cool, as we used to say, young people wanted to have a good time. Rock, long hair and drugs. We were thirsty for novelty, any sort of novelty. They called me the "New Age Surrealist". Why not? Surrealists lived outrageously. That was pretty much my philosophy. In no time, I became the leader of the Australian avant-garde. I was painting subversive stuff, oh yeah… I never favoured decorative arts over art. I hate decoration in all forms of art. Art isn't supposed to be ornamental.

The critics gave me a rough time, they were outright spiteful. My painting was too confronting for their petty conformist views. Oh yes, they found my work immoral, sick, obscene, revolting.

But my work challenged them. I know it did. They didn't like it and at the same time they couldn't help talking about it. They were annoyed, irritated, horrified, yet intrigued because I knew how to yield the existential angst lacking in this country. If you want my opinion, Australia is like a harp. It knows how to play the gleeful notes, how to celebrate a life of hedonism and sensuous pleasures. But this very harp is mute when it comes to expressing the low notes, a sense of gravity appended to the predicament of being alive. No tears here, no drama, no Cassandra.

See, my ambition was to paint the whole arpeggio... and my career is proof that I can. I've had huge exhibitions overseas. I had a major retrospective in Canberra last year. They even thought of making me a Living National Treasure. It's just a matter of time.

But experience doesn't help. Each time you start a new painting, you doubt. You doubt even more as you get older. I don't know how it happened, oh, might have been eight years ago, but one morning, I realised painting was too much of an effort and I couldn't go on. I went up to my studio, looked out to the forest, sat down on a chair and cried. I was old, so old. Death was around the corner, and I didn't know what to do about it, and I kept on crying... Then, something remarkable happened to me – Lucie. She was standing in the State Library and I saw in her the woman who would revive me, like some fresh-water spring. Yes, I suddenly realised how thirsty I'd been and for how very long; how much I'd turned into an old fart from living on my own, from being solely concerned with myself and my bloody painting. Yes, Officer Lawson, when I saw Lucie, life was given back to me. I was in awe. Her face, her hair, her complexion, her grace, her freshness. I had forgotten how beautiful women could be. It knocks you down. Their silky hair, their pencilled eyelids, the grain of their skin, their inviting cleavage. Lucie drove me mad.

She was on holidays in Sydney and I suggested that staying at my place would be cheaper than a hotel room. I drove her to Longland and we had the most exquisite time. I took her to the secret spots I've cherished since childhood, like the hidden paradise of Burning Palms Beach, where I took my first girlfriend. First kiss. I was fifteen. Beneath the same trees I kissed Lucie for the first time. The blue ocean roaring down the cliff hadn't changed. The thick green woodland creeping up the escarpment to the rocky ridge was the same. The king parrots and the rainbow lorikeets squawking in the trees offered a timeless sound. I was fifteen again.

Let's go on a pilgrimage, I said. Let's trace D.H. Lawrence's footsteps! Lucie could hardly believe that he had lived around here. The real D.H. Lawrence, she asked, the Lawrence of *Lady Chatterley's Lover*? I laughed and then I drove her to Thirroul. We gave each other our second embrace on the beach, that aphrodisiac beach, down below Wyewurk, the cottage where Lawrence and his wife Frieda had lived. This Frieda by the way, what a woman! After sunset, in homage to their freedom and their non-conformist lifestyle, I suggested a skinny dip. Lucie didn't get my meaning, but applauded the idea after I began stripping off my clothes. We jumped into the waves and danced beneath the full moon, uniting with the force of the earth and the infinite cosmos all around. It was ecstasy. I felt ageless. We returned dizzy from the sweet smell of the sand and the even sweeter smell of the ocean. That very same evening we made love as if there were no tomorrow. I wanted her so badly and she turned out to be the most delicate, the most caring of lovers. Her smooth fingertips running down my body... It was a kind of heaven and for two weeks we lived in harmony and closeness. My desire to be alive was renewed and the yearning to paint was coming back. It was as if the raven pecking at my heart had gone away. I've entertained a raven for many years, but that's another story...

I saw Lucie like some angel. Two weeks went by in no time. Lucie flew back to France as she'd planned to do. Shortly after, we began to write to each other. Her letters drove me mad. We also called each other. The more I listened to her adorable accent, the more I wanted her, and the more I knew she was the woman of a lifetime...

I can't bear the thought that she may have been harmed... You hear so many gruesome stories these days. The world is going crazy... Sorry, I'm not an emotional sort of man but I can't imagine my existence without her. I can't go on living without her. Thank you for your understanding, Officer Lawson.

The list of my guests? Certainly, you'll get it tomorrow... That's your number, right? I'll fax it first thing in the morning. I remain at your service. Naturally, I'll call at once if Lucie gets in touch with me, or if I remember any helpful details. Let me walk you back to your car. It's my pleasure... And do promise you'll come back in springtime, the garden looks like paradise.

Mathilde Sergent
Chemin des Dames
Pointilly
France

Sorry, whom am I speaking to? Inspecteur Agnelli of the Missing Person Department. And you're calling from Poitiers? My sister Lucie has disappeared? Yes, I know, I've already been contacted. I've also answered a few questions. The Australian Federal Police found my name in my sister's address book. First name on her list. I guess my sister remembers me when it suits her.

You really want to know what I think, Inspecteur Agnelli? I'm not at all surprised. One day Lucie is here, the next, whoosh, gone. When life gets tough, Lucie packs up and bails. Bye-bye. She's been doing it her whole life. She's changed cities. She's changed jobs. She's changed men. She's let her friends down. She's let her family down. As soon as she isn't happy with what she's got, she runs away instead of trying to solve her problems, or at least trying to understand what's wrong. Better hit the road and blame the whole world, including me, for her stuff-ups. Let me tell you one thing, Inspecteur Agnelli, I'm not going to worry myself sick over her.

No, I don't mince my words. But you can be sure that in a few weeks, she'll surface. I know it. What's wrong with her, you ask me, what's wrong? Everything, if you want to know! Clearly, you've never met Lucie. She suffers from a terrible illness called delusions of grandeur. At thirteen she pictured herself touring the world as a concert pianist. At fifteen she fancied becoming a writer. She studied and graduated in literature. That's how she ended up thinking she was better, smarter than everyone else. As if. Miss Know-It-All. She looked down on her family. Going to Australia, but what for? Why? Why do you have to go to Australia to give meaning to your life, honestly. Happiness is right under your nose, if you look hard enough for it. For God's sake, Australia! What a stupid idea... But let me tell you: if something serious happened to her, she probably asked for it. You see, Lucie is a carbon copy of our mother. She likes to play with fire and cries for help when she gets burnt. She acts impulsively and then, ouch! Too late...

That's right, I'm fourteen years older than Lucie and my sister Sylvia is ten years older than her. In a way, we grew up apart. Lucie was still playing with dolls when Sylvia and I were finishing high school. Lucie was different, withdrawn, read a lot, didn't speak much. I married early, at nineteen, and a year later I fell pregnant.

Pardon? What sort of relationship did Lucie have with my mother? Oh my! They were constantly battling it out. Mind you, my mother was a domineering woman and we all had to be at her beck and call. She manipulated everyone, including my father. Lucie ran away from home when she was underage. My parents had to send the police after her. She kept blaming us for what was wrong in her life... Truly, I can't understand her... She was well looked after, I can assure you. She had no reason to complain. My uncle, that is my father's brother, and my aunt took her in. They were besotted. They had no children. Lucie spent every single weekend with them, not counting summer and winter holidays. My parents didn't have the time to take us on holidays. They were too busy working... Yes, she was very well looked after, I would say. Our uncle was a teacher of literature and our aunt, who was also her godmother, a piano teacher. That's how she got her taste for books and music.

When she turned nineteen Lucie started to go out. She loved men and men loved her. She was pretty. I wouldn't say she was gorgeous, no, but she was pretty. And she knew it was an asset. My mother said she was a bitch on heat and she was right. She had affairs with married men, weirdos, slackers… I always wondered why she couldn't find herself a normal guy. No one was good enough for her. Is it so hard? She could have found herself an accountant or a teacher, had children, gone for bicycle rides on Sundays, and had holidays on the Atlantic seashore, like everyone else. No, too banal for her. Each time she had to dish up one of these weirdos. There's nothing wrong with a regular guy, is there? See, my sister Sylvia, she married a teacher and she is very happy with him. What's wrong with that?

Lucie's always been conceited, selfish and arrogant. She hasn't grown out of it. She unfailingly scorns our views. As a teenager, she was unruly, in rebellion against the family, against society, against what she called the *petits bourgeois*. But what's wrong with being a *petit bourgeois*? Our grandparents were shopkeepers who worked day and night, made good money, and helped their children get established. They weren't born with a silver spoon in their mouth. They tried hard to climb their way up the social ladder. What's wrong with that?

When was the last time we spoke to each other? Hmm… It could have been last year. She came with him, the partner. Arnold? Albert? No, sorry, I don't remember his name... Ernest! Thank you, yes, Ernest. It would have been September last year... Since then? No, as I've told you, we haven't been in touch since then... I organised a lunch here for Lucie and her partner. My sister Sylvia, her husband and two sons came along. Also present, of course, were my three children and their spouses. We were happy to see Lucie. Very glad. Glad, but sad too because our mother wasn't amongst us. She had passed away five months before. In May... Lucie didn't make the funeral.

As for him, the partner, I found him to be quite eccentric... a man that age with hair to his shoulders. A real cowboy with his leather hat and leather pants. After they left, my husband christened him John Wayne. That's what the whole family calls him now... If you want my opinion, I found him annoying. Nothing was grand enough for him, neither the amount of food, nor the car they'd hired. As he doesn't speak a word of French, we didn't get to talk much. Lucie tried to translate, but we quickly got tired of it and we carried on in French. I say, if you come to France, make an effort to speak our language, otherwise, don't complain... Lucie was proud of her John Wayne. She handed around the photos of their house, well, I should say, his house.

Honestly, I was staggered by her appearance that day. She seemed like someone else. She'd been to the hairdresser. She wore a silk dress, leather shoes – her wardrobe was typically limited to jeans and worn-out jumpers. She looked like a milady. I reckon she was trying hard to make an impression on me, but I wasn't impressed... I have a good husband and three wonderful children. My son is a pharmacist. He is thirty-five now and I'll be a grandmother again soon. My fourth grandchild. My youngest daughter is a veterinarian and the eldest is an international lawyer. She graduated at twenty-four. Twenty-four! That's unheard of. No need to prove anything... I married the man I met when I was eighteen, we've been together for thirty-eight years. We've never thought of divorce, wouldn't dream of it. With three children, our duty is to stick together. We support each other, as well as our family. My sister Sylvia is like me. She's happy with who she is. She lives in Poitiers and she didn't have to run away to Australia to find meaning to her life... I don't know if you understand, Inspecteur Agnelli, even though we are sisters, Lucie and I are like chalk and cheese. This happens sometimes in families...

Anyway, straight after lunch, Lucie and her partner drove off to Bordeaux. They could have stayed. They were very welcome. The most comfortable bedroom was ready upstairs. But they turned down my invitation. I couldn't understand why. My husband doesn't like Lucie. He never liked her... After they left he said that she finally got it right. She's not going to wind up like your mother, poor as a church mouse. At least we're off the hook and now John Wayne can look after her... I myself wasn't so sure if we *were* off the hook. Lucie thinks she's won the lottery with her five-star life and her famous artist, but I wonder how long it will last. My husband laughed. She thinks she's different, he said, but unfortunately she's like everyone else. He carried on, saying that when you don't want to conform to the norm, it's alright, as long as you have the financial or intellectual means to be different. But your sister Lucie, she isn't Rockefeller's daughter, and she hasn't got Einstein's brain. And that's why she's mad at the world. And when you are neither Rockefeller nor Einstein, you blend in and follow the flock like everyone else... He's so right. He knows life, my husband.

Yes, they drove here from Saintes. They hired a car at the train station; it's just a forty-five-minute drive to Pointilly. It is so beautiful here, hilly, green, we're surrounded by vineyards, and in autumn there is every shade of yellow and red. I immediately loved the place. A seventeenth-century manor house on twenty hectares of land... But, you know, we bought when all those run-down country houses were still affordable. No one wanted them. Too much work. Would you believe that the English and Dutch now buy them for a fortune? Back then the place was a ruin. An absolute ruin! Oh yes, Pointilly is beautiful and I am fond of it, even though it's a bit too far from the ocean for my taste. I adore the ocean. I would have loved a Tudor style mansion facing the sea. Just like in Biarritz. Oh well, one day maybe... I thought we should have a pool. All our neighbours have a pool. I told my husband, we've got to have one too. Come on, now we belong to the fiefdom of Grande Champagne, we've got to keep up! So, we had a pool built...

Huh? What happened to my mother? Oh, that's a sad story... See, she was a smart woman, but too ambitious. She ran a large real estate agency. She was very successful. Then her fortune dwindled away to nothing through bad investments and her own greed. Yes, she lost her mansion and the properties she inherited from both sides of the family. She sold everything down to her last ring. That was very sad indeed... My father? What can I say about him? He was a ghost, completely indifferent to the world. He watched the disaster unfold and, honestly, I don't think he gave a fig.

But don't get me wrong, we are a close-knit family. We meet up every year at Christmas, New Year and Easter, and when my mother was alive, she was invited to Pointilly, along with her new partner. Naturally, after my father's death, she got herself a new man... No, there are no outcasts in our family. Everyone gets a seat at my table. We are always glad to see each other. But when Lucie came back last September – supposedly to interview a musician, she was writing some book or article, don't ask me, I didn't get the full story – she really came back just to flash her John Wayne.

Lucie has always been jealous of me... As a matter of fact, I should say both my sisters have been jealous of me. Why? Because I did better than them. Do you know what they say behind my back, what they'd never say to my face? They say that I married money... Look, I met my husband when I was eighteen, as if I cared about money back then. He was good-looking and I liked him. One day he told me completely out of the blue that his father owned a vineyard in Grande Champagne. I was blown away. Grande Champagne! Gosh, the prized heart of the Cognac region. When his father died, my husband, an only child, inherited the house, the farm, the distillery and a fifty-hectare vineyard. We sold the house to buy a bigger one in Pointilly. My husband quit his job as an architect and converted to viticulture. No good to have people working for you if you aren't around... you've got to keep an eye on your business.

I've been lucky, so what? Why feel ashamed to be well off? Is it a sin to be rich? Let me tell you the truth, I feel no guilt living in a mansion. None. Oh yes, Lucie came here to play milady at the millionaire's arm, as if to say, see, this time, I'm not doing too badly... But I wasn't impressed with that Ernest. This time, I reckon, she's done a fine job at getting into trouble.

My gut feeling, to get back to where we started, is that nothing serious has happened to Lucie. I know my sister. She's more conniving than she appears. She's like my mother. She will reappear soon enough. Give her two to three months, and she'll call you from Mexico or Santiago...

Nicole Letourneau
Petersham
Sydney
New South Wales

Last time I saw Lucie was the Sunday before last, at the party. Did I notice anything? I certainly did. Lucie wasn't her usual self. I asked her if something was up. She shrugged. She said she'd been busy cleaning, she'd not had time to go to the hairdresser. I laughed: you don't need the hairdresser to look gorgeous, my *mignonne*. She sighed and said she'd been up since five... The catering staff had not shown up until the last minute. Yes, I think she was exhausted.

Ernest? Well, something wasn't right... The few times I came up to Lucie, he would spring out of nowhere. I got the feeling that he didn't like us talking to each other... Anyway, Lucie was busy with the guests, in and out of the kitchen, serving drinks, serving food, making sure everyone was happy. The waiters Ernest had hired lacked experience. They couldn't hack it. No, Lucie wasn't herself... Still she put up a good show, smiled a lot...

At one point, someone asked her to play and she sat down at the piano. She's usually much too self-effacing to perform to an audience. But there she was playing Chopin, Schubert, Mozart. Everyone was in awe of her virtuosity and beauty... in awe of this woman in a black evening gown... her hair tied up in a chignon... But I never got to find out what bothered her. I did notice that she was blunt with Ernest and on one occasion he scoffed: you're always right, honey, there is no point talking things over, you're such a smart one... I found him irritating.

How did I meet Lucie? By chance really, last January, at the Art Gallery of New South Wales. Lucie overheard me speaking French to my daughter June. She looked at me and asked if I'd been a student at Poitiers University. Not even close, I said. I'm from Paris, the Batignolles area. And I've never been to university... We laughed... Oh, the Batignolles, she replied, I remember a good bookshop on Avenue de Villiers. You look a lot like someone I know, she added. We talked for a while and swapped phone numbers. That's how we became friends.

I often call on her in Longland. Ernest doesn't let her drive his car, a vintage Chevrolet that costs a fortune to maintain. Lucie isn't used to driving on the other side of the road. That's what Ernest says, anyway. He drives her everywhere. Lucie is fed up with being constantly chaperoned. The train doesn't stop near Longland, so if you don't have a car, you are marooned in the valley. The closest train station is five kilometres up the road, at Watooga, and it is a very steep road. You wouldn't want to have to carry a suitcase up there... Each time I want to see her, I drive... Yes, I've spent a few weekends down there. Lucie has been lonely. Besides we're always glad to have a chance to speak French. Our community isn't large in New South Wales.

Uh-huh, that's correct, I didn't go to Ernest's party on my own... Rosy Barth drove me and my little girl June. Rosy? Well, I met Rosy in Kings Cross recently. She runs an art gallery. She sells Aboriginal art and I was looking for a dot painting for my mother's birthday. I found one at Rosy's, a small one, the only one I could actually afford. We realised that we'd both been invited to Ernest's party. We were spun out. It was a strange coincidence. We decided to go in one car. June insisted on coming with me to Longland. I wasn't keen but she cried so much that I gave in.

How was the party? Ooh... It was really over the top and outlandish, like in a movie. Around sixty people. Mostly artists. Misfits. Crazies. Borderlines. Yes, a truly different crew. They're fun. They don't freak me out. I'm used to being around eccentric people. My father is an artist. He lives in Paris.

The old artists' studios in Montparnasse. Next to the cemetery. That's where Alberto Giacometti and Marcel Duchamp worked. I met Christian Boltanski there... Quite an amazing encounter... Oh yes, the party panned out very well. Great music, good food, lots of booze.

Huh? Let me think... Yes, actually... Something happened. Late in the evening... Ernest had an argument with some stuck-up guy in a white tuxedo. They were talking art. Ernest only talks about art and he's always right. The snob called him a pornographer. It could have been funny, just a bad joke, but it got out of control. Ernest took it the wrong way and threatened to punch his lights out... I found it so embarrassing that I walked away. I didn't want to be a witness. Angry drunks make me feel uncomfortable and Ernest was very drunk and angry... Yes, Ernest runs on heavy fuel. Whisky, vodka, gin, anything he can get his hands on, he sculls... and when he's gone round the bend it can get messy.

Violent? Have I ever seen him be violent? No, I wouldn't say so... Acting stupid, yes, acting wild, yes. But, you know, I don't live with Ernest. And Lucie doesn't tell me everything...

From the sitting-room I heard the guy yell pornographer several times... You call yourself an artist, but you're no better than a pornographer! Ernest shouted back, you can stick pornography up your arse! People giggled. I had the feeling that everyone had been waiting for Ernest's outburst. The highlight of their week. Definitely something to talk about.

When I was about to leave Lucie invited us stay the night, but I said I'd go back with Rosy. June was asleep upstairs. We were the last guests to leave... Oh, could have been four, four-thirty. Yes, four-thirty... Did I see anyone else around? No, as I said, we were the last. I said goodbye to Lucie. I said goodbye to Ernest. He was as drunk as a lord. I don't even know how he managed to get up the stairs to his bedroom.

What do I think of Ernest? Hmm... Hard to say... Ernest is a great artist and a Casanova. His whole life revolves around women. Women and sex. The minute he saw me, he looked me straight in the eye. You have a very interesting face, he said. Would you like to sit for me? I looked straight back at him and replied, why not. I've posed many times for my father and his friends. When she was young my mother was a model in Paris, so I am no stranger to that world. And I was glad to make some extra money.

Yes, I sat for Ernest in his studio, up in that tower.

What a place! You haven't been in his studio? It's unbelievable! On the first floor, he has a small bed and a sink. He sleeps there sometimes. Then you find a narrow winding staircase that takes you to the second floor. That's where Ernest works. The studio is always locked up. There is no phone. Ernest doesn't want to be disturbed... Can you imagine a place with a glass pyramid for a roof, overlooking the forest? You see the tree-tops all around like a green ocean, rolling from the valley to the ridges of the hills that surround the house. In winter the mist rises up from the gullies. Sometimes the fog wraps the house up to the first floor. It gives you the impression of floating above a cloud. It's quite magical. And the smell is wonderful too. Such an inspiring place for an artist...

I like to go there with my daughter. It's healthier than living in Petersham. Just cars here, traffic noise and fumes. Still, I wonder why they built such a beautiful house in that dark hollow. Ernest told me once that the guy who built the house, a German if I remember correctly, was fond of rowing and fishing. He fancied having a lake and figured he could source water from a nearby creek at the bottom of the valley. Years ago, Ernest found a series of blueprints in the attic and that's how he worked out that the lake is artificial. In that grand old house the only spot to catch good light for painting is in the tower.

I've sat a dozen times for Ernest. He made two portraits of me, both in the nude. No, I've never seen them. Ernest doesn't show his work unless it's completely finished, and he paints very slowly. That's the Renfield technique. Very slow, very meticulous, small brush strokes. He mixes each colour, he never prepares them beforehand. He takes his time.

How did we go? You mean how did the sittings go? When Ernest asked me to lie on a leather couch, I recognised *the* red leather couch I'd seen in so many of his paintings... You wouldn't believe how important I felt. I realised I was going to be immortalised. Ernest Renfield is a renowned painter, you know. I didn't see his retrospective in Canberra last year, but I flicked through the catalogue. That's how I recognised the red leather couch... Anyway, it took him a long time to find the right pose. The arms this way. The legs that way... Ernest is very fussy. Then he stood behind his easel, prepared his colours. He looked so powerful, so manly, so impressive. He took a long breath. He was concentrating, silent, grave, staring at me, though at the same time not really looking at me, and then he started fighting with the work, growling, mumbling, sitting down on a stool, standing up. Such an imposing man, so tall and heavy, not young, and then he suddenly seemed lighter, moving like a ballet dancer. It went on for hours. I begged for a break. I was frozen to the bone. My legs were going numb. But Ernest put more wood into the stove; he didn't want a break. He kept on painting as if in a trance. Yes, very intense for both of us. He's a very passionate man.

So no, I didn't see the final product, but I saw the two he did of Lucie... A couple of canvasses were turned against the wall. One day, when he'd gone to the toilet, I quickly took a look. Honestly, I think you should check them out too, because they're kind of unsettling. And compared to the work I've seen in the catalogue, they're definitively not good portraits... Yes, both are nudes. How could I describe them? It looks as if Lucie's body is being pulled apart like a piece of meat, stretched like a vivisected toad pinned down on a board... I'm sorry, Officer Lawson, what I'm saying is gross... really gross, but that's the only way I can describe it.

I should also tell you that, well, Ernest tried his luck... He had a go, if you know what I mean... He put his brushes down without warning, walked up to me and fondled my breasts. I pushed him away. I'm not the sort of woman to open my legs on request. He got the message, believe me... No, of course I never told Lucie. She would have been hurt, especially after he announced he wanted to marry her. Can you imagine, if she knew about him trying it on with me? No, he tried twice before realising he was wasting his time.

Why did I call the police last Wednesday? Lucie and I got into the habit of calling each other on Mondays or Tuesdays. And last week she didn't call me. I found it unusual. Tuesday, I waited all day for her to give me a buzz. Wednesday, I called Longland and asked Ernest if I could talk to Lucie. Ernest said Lucie wasn't in Longland... That's why I called the police on Wednesday... Do I fear that something has happened? Yes, I do... Lucie isn't erratic, she's quite the opposite actually, she's a together person, and it's not like her to disappear without warning.

Paula Rieter
Cours de l'Intendance
Bordeaux
France

Yes, Lucie is my best friend, Inspecteur Agnelli. She's like a sister to me. You know, we haven't exchanged a bad word in twenty-four years... We always speak on the phone on Sundays. I call her every fortnight, sometimes every week, between nine and ten, morning here, evening in Australia... Just over a month ago, must have been Sunday 30 September, I remember that Lucie kept repeating she'd made the right decision... She sounded very cheerful on the phone. It seemed that her relationship with Ernest was going great. He's the kind of man who never runs out of ideas to keep one entertained. They'd driven all over New South Wales. One day off to the beach. The next to an art gallery. The following to a posh restaurant. Or the Opera House. Ooh, it sounded like she'd been having an incredible time.

It sounded like a fairy tale, Inspecteur Agnelli, but she hasn't contacted me in eight days; and I've been mulling things over. Eight days is a long time when you worry yourself sick for your best friend. And I'm gathering that perhaps life wasn't as great as she'd pretended it to be.

I've known Lucie for a long time. We met as first-year university students at Poitiers. When we last spoke on the phone, she didn't hint at any particular problem, but I've had a closer look at what she's written lately... Lucie writes, yes... She's been serious about writing for a while now. She's written articles for classical music magazines and she's had a go at novels, short stories and poetry. She started when she was a student in literature... I really think she's talented. No, her novels haven't been published, but she's persisting in finding herself a publisher.

About five months ago she sent me a short story she was about to submit to a literary magazine. As usual, she wanted me to read it before sending it... I've always been straightforward with her and she appreciates that... Anyway, I read it... Her story was macabre, just the opposite of what Lucie is. Yes, very dark and distressing. Her mother's death last year saddened her deeply... There was a terrible thing seeping up from that story that made my flesh crawl. After reading it, I immediately picked up the phone. I didn't bother checking the time difference. It might have been the middle of the night in Australia, I didn't care. I was worried, I had a very bad feeling. Is everything alright, I asked. She wouldn't open up. Lucie, talk to me, I said again, are you okay? She took on a reassuring voice, saying that she was fine. Everything was going well. She lived in a beautiful country. Yes, she said life was good over there. We chatted for a while longer. But still I couldn't piece things together. Her charmed life in fairyland and her dark story didn't match.

Then I worked it out... Yes, over the last eight days, I've become convinced that she's been deceiving me. Her entire tale has been a long-running lie... Look, she told me Ernest had driven her to a sunny beach to have a swim, right? I know she lives in Australia, still, winter is winter, especially in New South Wales. I watch the international weather report every day, and it's cold down there in winter. It doesn't make sense... When Lucie lived in Bordeaux, she wouldn't take a dip in the Atlantic Ocean on a hot summer day, she found the water too cold... And as for the art show, another lie... She said thcy had gone to the Rupert Bunny exhibition at the Art Gallery of New South Wales. I checked. Yes, I did... I wanted to be sure... I found out that the exhibition had closed before Lucie even moved to Australia. It doesn't add up, does it?

Ernest? Do I know him? Oh, yes, I do... I met him last September, when he and Lucie stayed here with me in Bordeaux. My flat isn't big but I have a spare bed in the lounge room. Joël Fargue, from

Les Editions Fargue, read Lucie's series of articles on the composer Olivier Messiaen and approached her to consider a biography of Jean Lucien. You might know of Lucien, the famous violinist from the Orchestre de Paris... He would be in his nineties now... He had made himself available to be interviewed by Lucie that September. Lucie was over the moon. Here was her chance to finally have a book published... It's almost impossible to get the attention of a Parisian publisher... They're like Olympian Gods. If you get to see or hear from one of them in your lifetime, lucky you!

Pardon? Ernest Renfield? What do I think of him? Well, at first, I was very impressed. Such a personality. Brazen, funny, charming, well read... The age difference? No, it didn't seem to be an issue. Besides, he and Lucie looked very much in love. At least, that's what I perceived. That being said, I only spent three days with them... I drove them to the ocean. We took walks on the beach. We ate mussels in a seaside shack. Ernest found that exotic. He was happy, yes, very happy, until the third day...

I drove them to the museum of contemporary art in Bordeaux. I love going there. I thought Ernest would too... But he got in a state when he saw Daniel Buren's palisade, and then later when he watched a video by Marc Alder. It's a museum of contemporary art after all... They were hosting a retrospective on the Arte Povera movement. Anyway, one look at that Kounellis and he flew into a fury, storming off. We hurried after him, ran up the street, caught up with him and apologised. I thought he'd have appreciated the place. This museum is highly regarded in France. But he kept on thundering... All this stuff is bogus, it doesn't induce any questioning or discomfort, it's a sham, wrecked cars piled up, dirty old jackets hung on a rusty hook! I cannot see art, but a bloody piano painted red or white or whatever colour the "conceptual artist" fancies. As for Marc Alder's videos? Oh, the videos. They're pure shit! The guy shoots the arse of a hippopotamus having a crap in psychedelic colours and that's it? That's what conceptual art is, a total con job consecrated by museums, art critics, the big shots and the market. Ha-ha, the market! He kept ranting and it was pointless trying to calm him down. People stopped to stare at us. I was mortified.

By the evening, he had calmed down. Lucie said he had a nap and felt better. He behaved in a pleasant manner during dinner. He didn't mention his fit of anger or apologise. I thought that was very rude... And they left Bordeaux the following morning. I drove them to the train station. They were going to Paris to meet Jean Lucien.

How did I feel when Lucie left France to live in Australia? Well, I encouraged her… I thought it was brave… Lucie's friends, her family, everyone was prompting her to leave. She'd broken up with a married man after a relationship of five years. He ran the typical dual life of a married man who cheats on his wife, pretends to go on work trips while spending the weekend with his mistress. He made a pledge to Lucie that he would eventually divorce his wife. His children were too young, maybe when the children had grown older, he'd speak up, pack his suitcase and go. Blah, blah, blah… Lucie waited. When the wife got wind of the story, she told her husband their marriage was over and asked him to leave, which he did. In his next move, he dumped Lucie… Some guy! She was devastated, but anyone could've guessed from the start their story wouldn't end well. Married men never leave their wives for their mistresses.

Lucie is a romantic. She believes in love. And each time she falls in love, that's it, she stops thinking straight. It's always marvellous, she always finds the man of a lifetime. But she's never had a happy love life. When she first met Ernest, Lucie hadn't completely recovered from her break-up with the married man. She was sick of Bordeaux, sick of her job and writing articles that required a lot of effort for very little money. She wanted to get away, to be by herself and dedicate more time to her writing. Yes, leaving France, I thought, would be good for her. You need guts to go to the other side of the world. I know I couldn't... Mind you, leaving was probably the best way to get away from her family because they're such a bunch of lunatics. I met them all one Christmas. Lucie was invited to her older sister Mathilde's and was reluctant to go on her own. We drove to Pointilly. Sylvia, her other sister, and her husband and children were there too. They were all very polite and well mannered but I could feel hatred between them.

Three times a year, at Easter, Christmas and New Year, Lucie was invited to Mathilde's. She always whinged about it, but always went. How many times have I tried to persuade her not to go? Each time you see them, it makes you sick, I would tell her. You know they'll hurt you, they'll drop some dirty comment you'll take to heart. Still, she would go. And each time she came back crying. I know it might sound terrible, but I reckon Lucie can't differentiate between love and hate... It sounds terrible but it's true... On the one hand, she's gets attached to people who blatantly harm her, on the other, she distrusts people who genuinely care for her.

See, she is the youngest of three girls. She's always claimed that her mother hated her, but it worked both ways. They always detested each other. True her mother very much cared for her two older daughters and shunned Lucie, who was an "accident". When her aunt and uncle, that is her father's brother, offered to have Lucie live with them, her mother was more than happy to unload the burden… So, in many ways, when Lucie decided to leave for Australia, it was an opportunity to break free from that farrago. She had found herself an outstanding man. She was going to live in a stunning place. What else could you want? I assumed she would be happy with Ernest, start a new life on new ground… That's what I thought, but neither of us could foreshadow what was in store. Who could?

The rain was pouring heavily the day she left France. We had lunch at my flat. I drove her to Merignac airport. Her plane for Paris was leaving in the afternoon. I gave her a copy of one of my favourite books, Sōseki's *Three-cornered World*. I'd wrapped it in gold paper. She was glad to leave and at the same time scared. We were both scared… We tried to talk but couldn't help crying… We didn't know whether we would see each other again. Australia is such a long way away. We stared at each other without a word and I saw in Lucie's eyes a glimmer of doubt. It was a risky thing to do. I'm strong, she said, I'll manage, as if she had read my thoughts. A voice called the passengers. First call. Second call. Lucie walked hesitantly through the boarding gate and disappeared. As soon as I left the airport, I burst into tears. I drove home miserable. I spent the next two days travelling with her, flying all the way through Europe, Northern India, South East Asia, having a cigarette at Singapore airport, flying across the equator to enter the Southern Hemisphere, gliding above the Australian desert... and I cried all the way with her. No, we didn't know what was in store. I can't figure out what happened to her. Eight days... I haven't had a proper night's sleep in eight days. I called my boss yesterday to let him know that I wasn't feeling well... I can't understand. Eight days... It's not at all like her.

Gary Whitehall
Paddington
Sydney
New South Wales

I left Longland around three o'clock in the morning... Yes, that's right, shortly after three... Did I see Lucie Bruyère then? No, she wasn't around... Did I talk to her throughout the evening? Yes, of course, we talked a lot, in fact. Each time she went outside to have a cigarette, we talked. I'm a smoker myself. We smoked a lot that night, so Lucie and I, we ended up chatting a lot.

What did we talk about? We talked about cleaning. Yes, cleaning. Lucie kept looking at the glass doors, as if she was looking for some speck of dirt on the panes of glass. She looked tired, edgy, and said it had taken her four weeks to tidy up the house and the garden. Luckily, she'd found a local cleaning lady to give her a hand. I frowned. Ernest could have hired people to get the job done, but he didn't. No surprises there. I know Ernest, he doesn't like strange faces around the place. He can easily get paranoid and most of all, he can be stingy. He was certainly glad to have saved a few bucks on the cleaning... Anyhow, Lucie said it was worth the effort. I agreed. A dozen small, round tables draped in white satin had been set around the reception room, with a posy of white asters clumped in the middle of each. It looked nice, fresh, welcoming…

What else did we talk about? Nothing of consequence. Just small talk… Have I known Lucie for long? I met her shortly after she moved to Australia. About two years ago. She and Ernest came to Sydney one Saturday morning, yes, it would have been two years ago, they were going to lunch at a new seafood restaurant at the Wharf, yes, that's when I met her for the first time. When it comes to eating and drinking, Ernest doesn't mind splurging. I heard a husky voice yelling from the doorstep: Gary, old pal, why don't we organise an exhibition, an unforgettable one this time? I turned around, it was Ernest. He was fired up. He seemed to have got his mojo back. Yes, I could see he was keen to jump back into the ring, but still I couldn't work out why. I understood when a good-looking woman walked in and Ernest, beaming, introduced Lucie. He looked really smitten. Unlike his previous girlfriends, she didn't seem the bombastic sort… I thought she could be the right woman for him. She could prompt him back to painting. I was instantly fond of her. I shook her hand, then clasped Ernest's, saying, I am with you, old chap, that's good news, and it's time you did. He nodded. His hand was shaky. We could read each other's minds. I was glad for him. He had been on his own for too long. I was also waiting for him to get back to serious painting. He'd wasted the last fifteen years recycling old ideas. As for his latest works, honestly, I didn't have a clue. He always keeps me in the dark. I'm his art dealer and I hadn't seen a canvass in six years. I'm patient but, still, six years is a long time...

Now talking about the Sunday of that party, Officer Lawson, I wish to mention something that's been bothering me. It's related to Lucie's brooch. Sunday before last was a cold day. A nasty wind picked up at nightfall. The temperature suddenly dropped. Each time Lucie went outside to have a smoke... Where outside? Well, on the front terrace, that's where we stood throughout the evening. Each time she stepped outside, she would put her jacket on. A tweed jacket. She'd pinned a brooch on her lapel. I knew the brooch very well since I'm the one who sold it to Ernest. It's a small, silver cut-out, about three centimetres long, of a Magritte painting called *The Lovers*. It has been reproduced many times in posters and postcards. Let me describe it, I'm sure you'll recognise it... Two heads side by side, shrouded in a white cloth, light enough to let the protruding features of the faces jut out. The nose. The chin. You guess easily it's a man and a woman. The two faces look… Now, hang on a minute, because Magritte did several versions of this painting… In one of them the couple looks in the same direction and in another, they are kissing, so they face each other. Look, I don't actually remember which one I sold to Ernest. See how poor my memory is… Anyhow, three years ago the Art Gallery of New South Wales had a Magritte retrospective and I got the fancy, God knows why, of having these distasteful Magritte brooches, cups, key-holders, tee-shirts and baseball caps on display at my gallery. Tourists love this kind of junk. As for this particular brooch, well, to be honest, I hated it. The painting is vivid with contrast, but this silver-grey cut-out is creepy, yes, I found it quite morbid. Ernest spotted the damn thing in the window and claimed he loved it. Are you serious? You want to buy that? I asked. He snatched the brooch and lobbed it on the counter. Who are you giving it to? I persisted. To the woman of my dreams, he replied… Anyway, while Lucie and I were dragging on our cigarettes, I couldn't wrench my eyes away from that brooch. Eventually I looked at Lucie, I looked at this woman in the prime of her life…

I hadn't seen much of her since she had moved in with Ernest. She and Ernest have come to my gallery five or six times in the last two years, and once I organised a lunch in Rose Bay, where I live. My mother came along, delighted to meet the famous Ernest Renfield. Ernest had been living like a hermit since he had moved back to Longland twelve years ago. He stopped throwing parties like he used to. And although I never failed to send him invitations to my shows, it was pointless, he never came...

Now before I forget, let me tell you another thing that has been bugging me, something to do with an ashtray. As I lit my first cigarette of the evening and looked around, I mean, when I was on the front... Yes, that's right, the terrace overlooking the lake... I wondered where I could stub out my cigarette. I was about to go inside to fetch an ashtray when Lucie, red in the face, apologised, and said, I'll get you an ashtray. But she never brought me one, busy as she was with the other guests. On top of that, Raphaël, Ernest's brother, was buzzing around her like an annoying wasp. I think he is enamoured with her. That evening, he gave her his number, then later his address, saying she was welcome to stay with him anytime should she come to Queensland. Lucie was clearly embarrassed. To avoid him, she constantly came out onto the terrace to take a few puffs with me before returning to the party... Each time Lucie stubbed out a cigarette she attempted to brush away the ashes with her shoe, or sometimes with her fingertips, until she thought all the evidence had been carefully cleaned away. Then, she would pick up the cigarette butt to stash it behind the bronze Cupid standing on the side of the terrace. You might have seen it when you went to Longland, it's Ernest's early metalwork. The statue is hollow at the back, and that's where Lucie disposed of her cigarette butts. With Raphaël becoming painfully insistent, Lucie wasn't paying much attention to me. By mid-evening she spotted my stubs at the foot of the balustrade, turned pale and fell into a panic… She ran inside, hurried back with a plastic bag and started to collect them. I apologised, of course, feeling terribly embarrassed… As I was assisting her in gathering up the stubs, I noticed she kept glancing anxiously through the glass door, like some disobedient child afraid to be found out. Now she was tossing her own cigarette butts into the bag. She forced a smile, then squeezed the bag into a tight little ball and dashed to the kitchen. Her behaviour struck me as unhinged. At that moment, the two shrouded faces of Magritte's lovers crossed my thoughts and curiously, they made me think of Ernest and Lucie… Lucie and Ernest…

I walked across the terrace and stood behind the glass door to look inside. Ernest was slumped in his large wing chair. His eyes were half-closed, his mouth in a twisted pout. Was it contempt? Conceit? Boredom? I know that man so well... The renowned painter, the braggart who'd got himself a new trophy wife, the old lecher raising his glass to Rosy, now belly-dancing around his chair... It all made me feel ill at ease... It was a wild party, believe me. Such eccentric guests, everybody dancing, braying, laughing, drinking, smoking, snorting, oh yes, they were doing drugs. Honestly, this crowd looked like cardboard cut-outs moved by an invisible hand. That shadow theatre was grotesque and even frightening. And to think how much I loved going out when I was younger. But that night I felt very much out of place...

I stepped away from the glass door in dread. I've known this fool of a man for too long, I thought. I'm sixty-five; we've known each other for forty years. We met as students at the Sydney School of Fine Arts. We graduated and were appointed as lecturers there. I wanted more from life than a mapped out academic career and decided to establish my own art gallery. I started with a small showroom in Potts Point. Ernest was the first artist I contracted and his early exhibitions were a flop. I persisted because I believed in him, because his work was revolutionary. Back in the Sixties the mainstream artists slogged away at still-lifes, you know apples, flowers, and also at bushscapes, the standard gum trees and billabongs. But Ernest's work spoke to me intimately...

You might get a clearer picture if I told you that my birth name is Gavril Goszyński, born to Polish parents in the Soviet Union. By 1933 my father had understood what was in store for the Polish Jews. My parents didn't dither any longer and fled Lubán in December 1933. They tried their best to convince their relatives to leave Poland as well and seek refuge in Russia, but no one listened... Between January and June 1942, my grandparents and my relatives, both sides of the family, were rounded up. My grandparents died in Treblinka, my cousins in Birkenau... I was born in Moscow and after the war my parents opted for Australia instead of America. We came here as refugees.

As a young man, I could not express the tragedy of my family through my own art. My parents never talked about what happened to our family, their silence was laden with the remorse of being alive. My own childhood was peopled by ghosts. Ernest's work unravelled my anxiety and somehow helped me face the demons.

Back then Ernest was the most extraordinary young man and everyone wanted to be his friend.

He was handsome, eloquent and witty. The Renfields are an old family. His great grandparents owned the collieries in Kiama. Three generations of Renfields have lived in Longland. They carried a proud conceit about their wealth, they were also very conformist. I remember spending a weekend in Longland for Ernest's twenty-first birthday. His old-fashioned mother, poor thing, who looked like she was wearing a corset beneath her thick black dress, walked right up to me and asked before saying anything else: do you believe in God, Gary? I was taken aback. I racked my brain in search of the right answer. Well, my parents never lectured me about religion, and for a long time, even at twenty-two, I had no idea about what being a Jew actually meant. I finally muttered, yes, ma'am. That was enough to make her happy and she said with conviction, that is very good, don't ever forsake Him, Gary. She never questioned me on matters of faith again. Looking back, I think it was an absurd situation.

Ernest's first paintings were rather satirical, almost grotesque. In the vein of German expressionism. He didn't hold back. The European tragedy was so far from his own experience and yet, he depicted the drama my family had left behind. Holocaust. Ruin. Devastation. He gave form and colour to a tormented story that was my own. He painted my own devastated homeland, my own decimated family.

Anyway, after three years of hard work it so happened that an influential art critic walked past my tiny showroom one evening. Two days later, the exhibition was given a half-page rave review in the *Sydney Morning Herald*. The artist Ernest Renfield was born. And not long after that, the show at the MOMA, the cover of *Time*... Things happen in a funny way in the art world. The fireworks can peter out very quickly but this one kept on going.

But I've gone off on a tangent, sorry, let's get back to the point... Lucie had gone to the kitchen with her plastic bag. Her behaviour perplexed me... I looked out to the forest. The wind had eased off. The full moon lit the sky. The mist hovered over the lake, which resembled a slab of heavy, cold lead. The clouds drifted in the moonlight... Suddenly the music stopped... They had been playing jazz, but now I could only hear the rustling and crackling of the forest. The woods are so dense, so dark, like a jungle closing in on you and there is no track. It's impenetrable, hostile, with creepers, lantanas and towering tree-ferns. It's oppressive. Shadows floated on the lake... And I felt presences... Not one presence but several. The music came back and

I went inside.

Ernest was still in his wing chair playing up as Ernest Renfield, the living myth. He was arguing with Fernando Sigotti. Sigotti is Ernest's nemesis. Twenty-five years ago Sigotti reviewed one of Ernest's exhibitions for the *Herald Sun*. He compared his work with that of Egon Schiele. Ernest loathes the suggestion that Schiele had ever influenced him. But Ernest doesn't let go and it only takes a few drinks for him to forget good manners. I moved closer. It can be entertaining watching Ernest. Let's face it: the man is an untamed beast who doesn't fit in a civilised world. He will never fit in it...

It was very late. People were sitting in a large circle around Ernest, who appeared wasted. The conversation was heated and all of a sudden the jesting got out of hand. Ernest got to his feet, hauling his bulky body out of his armchair, God knows how, and once up, he drawled: I'm no pornographer, you puritan tosser! I paint women's beavers, fuck women's beavers and I love it! Next minute he called Sigotti a motherfucker, before raising his fist. Sigotti stepped back and groaned: you are mad, Renfield, completely mad, you should be locked up or on medication!

This was the perfect opportunity to take my

leave... I quickly slipped away to the library and grabbed my duffle-coat. I waved goodbye to Ernest. He stared at me for some time. I don't think he recognised me. Then he gave a lurch before sinking back into his chair. I looked about. As I couldn't see Lucie, I left... As I said, it would have been about three o'clock.

Act II

Ernest Renfield
Longland
New South Wales

I didn't expect you so early in the day, Officer Lawson. Come inside, please... I feel wretched! Lucie's been gone now for sixteen days. Sixteen days!

I don't get it. Why hasn't she called me? Where is she? What have I done? Don't stand there, you'll catch a cold, come in, let's go to the kitchen. I was having my breakfast...

Sorry? Say that again? You'd like to go through Lucie's personal papers? Sure, Lucie's papers, why not? This way, Officer Lawson... To the left and down the corridor. Be careful, the passage is full of antiques... Watch that statue, the stand is wobbly. It's Medusa, that's an exceptional piece. I bought it many years ago from Lord Edward, a compulsive gambler. When he needed cash, he'd sell one of his treasures. Poor Lord Edward, he wound up selling what he'd collected over a lifetime. Rarities. Exceptional pieces. Everything!

Here we are. Warmer here, isn't it? Please take a seat. Coffee maybe? A tea? A drop of something? No? No alcohol? That's right, you don't drink. If you don't mind, I'll lace my coffee with rum. A rum toddy.

I beg your pardon? Ah yes, that's right, you wanted to go through Lucie's papers... I talk too much. You'll find her things as she left them, on the table over there. She prefers being in the kitchen, next to the fire. But it's all written in French. Good luck understanding it, it's all Greek to me! Please, go ahead. You have authority to do so... Yes, that's where she'd sit.

Do you know that as well as articles she writes poetry? Poetry! What a waste of time! People don't read poetry these days. Apart from the tabloids the rabble aren't interested in reading anything... least of all poems.

Anyway, why is she doing this to me? I've been like a father to her. And now, where is she? How is she managing without me? I'm here to provide for her, I was here to help. Why can't she be happy? How lucky she should be to have me, because when it comes to money, she's useless. And as for practical stuff, it's completely beyond her...

What do I mean? Ah, I can see that you've never met Lucie... So many examples come to mind, I don't even know where to start... Let's talk about her French publisher if you want, yes, this Fargue. Things were not going so well with him. No, not at all. If I hadn't got involved, she would've signed a dodgy contract. She'd agreed to start a job without laying down the terms of work and payment. You've got to stand up for your rights, I told her. You've got to learn to talk things through, Little Miss. And then, upon my word, Lawson, she looked at me and rolled her eyes, yes, she rolled her eyes... She should be grateful to have me supporting her. What about the piano over there? Yes, that's Lucie's piano. Do you play, Lawson? No, of course... No time. You're a busy man, like me... Well, the piano! That's another story! Boy, Lucie hadn't been here less than a week when she began to moan that she couldn't live without music. Alright then! I totally understood. Music is important to her. For me, music is nothing more than disturbing noise. Birdsong is the only music I can bear... Anyway, she wanted a piano. I drove her all over the state to find the special kind she wanted. If you want to hire a piano, that's fine with me, I said, but it's only fair you pay for it. She was a bit surprised but agreed.

Let me tell you, Lawson, I've seen better days... I have to be honest, I don't have money to burn. When I was at the pinnacle of my career, when I had exhibitions in every state, when none of my paintings were left unsold, when I was courted by merchant bankers and generous patronesses of the arts... Mind you, I've had a magnificent retrospective in Canberra last year but there was no money in that and these days, every cent counts. This house is costing me a fortune to run. I know... I know what you're going to tell me. But you've got to understand, Lawson, when Lucie moved to Australia, I assured her I would look after her, that's true. You're here to start a new life and be happy, I told her. Word for word, because that's what I genuinely felt. Yet the cost of living keeps going up... I don't think she realised that sooner or later she would have to contribute.

But you know, paying for the piano wasn't so much a matter of money. Let me explain... She was bored. That was obvious enough to me. Lucie was bored in Longland. To pass the time she rang France, or talked endlessly over the phone to her friend Nicole. Her nattering was so annoying – yack, yack, yack. Anyway, one morning I spotted a notice pinned on the community board in Watooga. *Immediate Start*, it said. A fashion store needed a shop assistant, part-time, nothing exhausting, and only five kilometres up the road. I would've driven her to work. I mentioned the notice to Lucie. It would've been perfect for her, but she brushed the idea aside. I was annoyed...

So, talking about the piano, well, I considered

it to be a luxury. We went north, south, west. We ended up hiring one from Jeff McCarthy's store in Moss Vale. He's in the phone book. He'll tell you the whole story himself, if you ask him. When Jeff heard Lucie play on one of the basic uprights, he was so impressed that he insisted she rent out a better quality piano for the same price. We shook hands on the deal. Yes, she played every day. She plays well, oh yes, very well...

Sunday? You mean the Sunday of the party? At what time did the last guests leave? I thought I'd already answered that question, Officer Lawson. They left at the crack of dawn. I'm up each morning at sunrise. It's the best time of the day to paint because of the light. Yes, the last guests left at dawn.

Interesting... You've been told that I was intoxicated... that I didn't know my head from my arse? Good grief! Why don't people mind their own business? I drink... That's what you heard. Well, I am a bit of a boozer, that's correct. I do drink. But before you speculate any further, let me tell you that I'm not an angry drunk. I'm a crying drunk. Drinking helps me not to think too hard on the human condition and forget about my own decline. Look at me! I've been adored, celebrated, praised, awarded, revered, given medals... They've organised dinner parties for me with the governor, at Government House. I'll be a national treasure soon enough. But I swear to you, in the end, it's all bullshit. "Fame is the mourning of happiness," Madame de Staël said. She was too right, the old bird. Just look at me... What do I have to show for all my achievements? I'm an old fart feeling sorry for myself, waiting for my damsel to call...

Remember the tight-rope walker of Nietzsche? In *Zarathustra*? No? You've missed out, it's one of the greatest books ever written... Imagine a guy walking on a rope stretched between two towers above a crowded market place. It's all going fine for him, he's carefully stepping ahead, when suddenly a jester jumps out from one of the towers. He follows the tight-rope walker, shouting "Get out my way!" As you would expect, the funambulist loses his balance and falls to the ground. As he is about to die, he asks Zarathustra, sitting by his side, if the devil will drag him to hell. And this is where the story becomes unsettling... Zarathustra tells him there is *nothing* to fear. There is *nothing*, Officer Lawson, after death, the after-life is a wide empty space. So why should we carry any fear since there is no devil, no soul, no paradise and no hell?

Let me tell you more about Nietzsche... Poor old Friedrich! He roams around Switzerland and

Italy. Imagine him in Sils Maria. He rents a room in a boarding-house. Cheap lodgings, flophouses, that's all he can afford. His old suitcase in a corner and that threadbare black suit hanging on a hook. On a table is a tray stacked with a dozen phials. His body is a mess. He's going blind. He's going deaf. He has migraines, fragile nerves, insomnia, lazy bowels, haemorrhoids... He can't drink wine, not even tea! He's a small guy, with a slight stoop, a funny old bachelor whose books don't sell. No one has ever heard of him. He is estranged from Wagner, his only friend. Meanwhile Lou Andréa Salomé, the one woman who might alleviate his solitude prefers another man. A better-looking one.

Nietzsche keeps writing... ten hours a day. He'll have to pay to get the last part of *Zarathustra* published. He knows he's a genius. He knows writing is his salvation. He doesn't know that he's going to spend the last twelve years of his life in darkness... It happens one day in Turin... He is watching a horse being mercilessly flogged by his owner. He rushes over, throws his arms around the horse's neck, and there and then he loses his mind. Yes, his power of reasoning disappears... Yes, he goes mad... Anyone in such a state of loneliness and wretchedness would lose their mind. Anyone! Forget about the horse, forget about the syphilis, forget about the misery, what drove him mad is the world's indifference... By 1900 he would be the most read and discussed philosopher of the time. The most *read* and the most *dead* philosopher of his time!

See, Officer Lawson, Nietzsche's work has been my gospel since I was eighteen. I never believed in God. My parents dragged me to church each Sunday, but the bloody rigmarole bored me to tears. It didn't make sense. Up you stand! Down on your knees! The Renfields had to be seen in church. My mother would only receive the Host after a thorough confession, after she thought she'd dusted every nook and cranny of her soul... They didn't go to church because they were good and righteous, no... The way they shafted their servants wasn't righteous at all... Did they ponder ashamedly over their sins, beseeching forgiveness? No, every week at mass they prayed for their collieries to yield better returns in the forthcoming year. They badgered God once a week because church was a bargaining place. Yes, church on Sunday and hating thy neighbour as thyself on any other day of the week... God is a tale for the dreamers and the retarded.

Still, I wish there was nothing to fear, Officer Lawson... But every so often I can feel a fucking jester trying to make me trip over, shouting at me:

lazybones, smuggler, pale-face, you ought to be locked up! He's been trailing me even closer since Lucie ran away...

Between you and me, I thought she loved me. Men are so easily fooled and old age turns them into blubbering imbeciles. Yes, I thought she was in love with me... Come a bit closer, Officer Lawson, I wish to display the most intimate details of my life, since I guess you are after the naked truth... Yes, see, the way we fucked, Lucie and I... Women, you wouldn't think they'd lie when they love a good fuck as she did. Because she loved it, I'm telling you... I know they are damn liars. It's in their blood, trying to con you, but when you're screwing, who do they think they're fooling? I know she wasn't fooling me. She was giving herself to me and she loved it. She came all the way across the world to be screwed by me... And now, she's gone. She's off to where? She's found a younger shag. You might want to ask my brother Raph. He'd have an idea. I saw him wooing her. Bloody Raphaël, he would do anything to wreck my life, even pinch the new bride from under her husband's nose... Anyhow if that's what she wants, good riddance. She can fuck off!

You want her papers? Be my guest, grab the lot! Take anything that might remind me of her. I don't want to hear any more about that bitch!

Lucie… Bloody slut! Where are you? Sixteen days. I've lost sleep. She doesn't realise. If only she could understand what she's putting me through. Let me tell you something: she never liked me. She came here to find a roof, to live off a sucker. She came, made herself comfortable and I gave her what she needed. She was looking for a sugar daddy who'd provide an easy life… Take everything! Please clear the table! I'll give you a garbage bag. I don't want to look at her shit anymore. She's killing me. Soon there will be nothing left of me but bitterness, resentment, impotence. You understand, Officer Lawson?

Look it's only eleven o'clock, and I'd like to stay here all day with this bottle of rum. Life isn't bearable if you don't blunt its sharp edges. But I should go back to painting, really, I'd be better off in my studio. I just haven't got the energy. I don't give a shit anymore. Lucie is killing me. Life is killing me. Honestly, isn't life killing you? I bet you have a lovely wife… and two fine kids. I bet you love your wife and relish playing cricket with your sons down at the park on Sundays. They're such good boys. The younger one wants to be a doctor, the older is studying to be a lawyer, someone standing up for lost causes like his daddy. Good on him! I haven't any children. I never wanted to father a child, to have to look at another version of myself. Ugh!

Yeah, take all of her papers! Her bloody poetry! Here is the bin bag. I don't want to see any trace of her. Good riddance and thanks for clearing up the mess! Do you mind if I don't walk you back to your car? I feel a bit gone...

Raphaël Renfield
Eight Mile Plains
Brisbane
Queensland

Has Lucie Bruyère been in touch with me? Yes, I did give her my number... Do you really think Lucie hides out at my joint? Sorry, boss, she isn't here... Bit of a shame, Brissie is a nice place, warm and sunny. She'd love it here.

Forget Renfield, people around here call me Raph. And Longland is another planet. I pissed off as soon as I could and been in Brissie for the past twenty-eight years. Sunnybank Motorbikes, that's me! And I'm fine where I am, thank you!

What sort of relationship do I have with my brother? Really want to know? Your ears will bleed... I hate the guy. Yep, hate's the right word. I hate his guts. So? Why did I drive all the way from Brissie to his fucking party? Why not? He sent me an invite. We hadn't talked to each other in donkey's years. Maybe time to patch things up... He's not that young. I thought it'd be a shame to pass up a chat before he croaked...

How did I feel going back there? Like shit. Why? Because I grew up in that house and the joint is mine as much as his. When I walked in I got a massive shock… The downstairs rooms hadn't changed… My mother loved having a rest in the sitting-room or the library. The tower was my father's getaway. My old bedroom was on the first floor, last one on the right, the corner room facing the lake. Ernest's room was on the opposite side of the house. Better that way.

Yeah, going to Longland, being back home and feeling like a stranger at my brother's place was a real downer. The wallpaper, the antiques, the knick-knacks, even the smell was the same. Ernest has just stacked up more stuff in twelve years, expensive stuff. I could see that much. Thinking of the past was hard to take.

Our parents died twelve years ago, just months apart. I wanted to sell the property but Ernest didn't. So he organised a valuation and bought me out of Longland. I got my half and I've since blown it. Moolah doesn't last. I've nothing to show for it while Ernest owns that grand house and acres of land… Ernest is Ernest… We've never liked each other. There's always been bad blood between us. Since the day we were born we've fought. As a kid, he was mean to me. At thirteen he was already built like a brick shithouse. One day he split open my upper lip. You know I've still got the scar…

So I did drive all the way to his party, Officer

Lawson. Yeah, I did. I hoped he'd changed. Hoped that this time we'd be able to talk to each other. Forget it! He walked up to me and barked, how nice of you, Raph. We shook hands. Cold as ice. Just by the way he shook my hand, I knew I'd made a mistake coming back. His whole court was prancing around, green-haired crackpots, tattooed dykes, bum-bandits. Jesus Christ, what a mob! And then this girl swanning around in the middle of them, this Lucie Bruyère you're talking about, Ernest's latest plaything.

What did I think of her? Not much... When I saw her flouncing about, I said to myself, here's the new trophy. Ernest's into collecting. He started with insects as a kid. Pinned them alive. Then he moved on to stamps, keyrings, foreign coins, tin soldiers and miniature cars. Wasn't long before he got a taste for collecting sheilas, mostly sluts, picked them up in bars, parties, at the beach. He liked the foreigners. He started with the Wogs and the Poms, then he landed a Frog. Lucie's a good catch for Ernest, a pretty one. At first glance, I thought, this one's a bit too good-looking to be smart. But we got yacking when she was having a smoke outside and she was smarter than she looked.

Huh? What did we talk about? I asked her what she was going to do in this shithole. There isn't much to do around there, unless you like watching birds. She told me she was writing the life-story of a French musician. I asked a few questions. It was all pleasant enough, until she started asking about the names of the people who'd lived here before. Well, the house and the land belonged to my family, I said. She carried on, saying, no, I'm not talking about your family, but the people who lived here before, I mean before the whites came here... What are you talking about, I asked. What do you mean *whites*? My olds got the house and the land from their olds, if that's what you want to know. That's not what she was asking, she said. She was talking about the Aborigines. You mean the blackfellas, I said, a bit stunned. Yes, what were they called, she wanted to know. How would I know their bloody names, they're Abos, that's all! What do you want to know that for? She reckoned she was interested in their music and painting, that sort of stuff, if you get my drift. And then she tells me she hasn't met a black since she's been in Australia. I laughed my head off! It's not around here you'll find them blackfellas. You've got to drive up north for that. Come to Brissie with me, you'll see truckloads of blackfellas up there. My ex, Terry, nice chick, she's an Abo.

You know, Officer, foreigners, they're all the

same. They walk around town thinking they'll bump into Abos playing the didgeridoo. And they don't. And they wonder why! She sounded like a real drongo. It's the twenty-first century. Hello? Wakey, wakey! Foreigners, they have no fucking idea...

What else did we talk about? Not much. Still I couldn't see what she was doing with Ernest. This chick, I thought, she's too good for him...

Huh? Why do I say that? Because I haven't a good thing to say about my brother and I'm not the only one... My parents wrote him off... When he came back from New York, he was out of control... My father went berserk... Why? Old stories, ask him if you really want to know. But Ernest is a weirdo...

Twenty years down the track his paintings were selling like crazy. The fucking art dealers asked him to paint shitloads of naked babes. He spat them out like a machine-gun. That wasn't smart. His work went off. I know... I've been told. But he was hungry for the loot, the sheilas, to be on top of the ant-heap... You can say he's some kind of a lunatic... Years ago, he decided to go to the museum every day, don't know which one, a big one, to copy a gross picture. Yeah, disgusting! He's got it upstairs in his studio. It's a woman's muff! He spent an entire month staring at a cunt. Nothing's missing. Each hair, each bit of rosy flesh...

No, I've never seen it. He just told me. He was proud of his feat. It's up in the tower. The bunker is always locked. He keeps the key on a string around his neck. You didn't know? Shows you how sick he is! I wonder what he does with this revolting painting. If he jerks off just looking at it...

The girls who sit for him? You know what? He just wants to have a good perve and hump them straight after they've sat for him. You didn't know, eh? He's a crowd-puller, Officer... You paint a woman's muff, that's the easiest way to make money and people love it. That's what the world wants to get a load of, the hairy pit...

Huh? Me? Jealous of him? Get real. Why would I envy him? I've got a good life here in Brissie. Queensland is the best place on earth. I'm not jealous, I just hate his guts. At least I'm honest enough to speak my mind. When my business wasn't going great and I asked for his help, he didn't lift a finger to get me out of the shit. He hides in his rock hole like a big fat crab waiting for the next morsel of prey to swim past.

Why do I say that? You ask him... He's such a smug bastard. And the girl, I kind of liked her when she was having a smoke outside, but you know what, I don't feel sorry for her. She's a lost soul, bored to tears in godforsaken Longland. We had a good chat. I made her laugh. That was quite an achievement seeing she didn't look that cheery for a chick about to get engaged.

Maybe I got it all wrong, but that's what I gathered when I saw he'd given her a ring. Nothing flash. Well, she didn't look that thrilled, the poor darl'. I've seen these girls in and out of Ernest's life. Truckloads of them. Why would you want to be with a guy like Ernest? You've got to be a bit of a crackpot yourself to want to hang around with that nutter. Ernest hasn't got any respect for women. He doesn't love women. He doesn't love anyone. He hasn't got what it takes to love.

Rosy Barth
Kings Cross
Sydney
New South Wales

Ernest's partner? What about her? Jealous of me? Well, she did give me the cold shoulder... Hang on a minute, what are you getting at? Nothing to do with me... The darling was angry because that night Ernest had his eye on other women. And yes, he did look at me too. I'm not over the hill just yet. He and I talked about the good old days, when we were in love...

Of course, I knocked him back! I'm not that sort of woman. I'm a married woman. I have three children. I told him to cut the flirting... Ever thought about retirement, I joked. He laughed. Retire from what? Rosy dear, it's in my blood... Ernest can be good fun when he's drunk. I also had a bit too much to drink...

No, I didn't go to Ernest's party to revive some old passion. No way! I went because I wanted to meet her, yes, I wanted to see the Venus in the flesh. That's what I call her, the Venus... Tall, stylish, well-spoken. But, you know, I don't think this French girl is actually Ernest's type. He always preferred Rubenesque women. He loves Callipygian Venuses, as he calls them... He finds them more inspiring...

Anyway, when I saw Ernest ogling every young woman at the party, I thought, Lucie dear, I give you six months... Huh? Yes, that's right... Ernest and I spent a few moments in the sitting-room... He cornered me... He pushed me in there as I was going to the bathroom, and shut the door. What time? How would I know?

He wanted to know what I thought. Of what, I asked. Of her, he responded. I laughed. It's not what you think, he said very seriously. I want to marry her. I shook my head. He got upset, really upset. You reckon I'm unable to make a woman happy? But you were happy with me Rosy, weren't you? I said, of course I was. Say it again louder, he demanded. I foolishly played along and repeated the words *I was happy with you!* I wished him good luck with his new girl. He picked up on my cynicism and accused me of jealousy. Well, perhaps it's true, I am a little jealous. Especially when he comes up close and pinches my cheek and says with that radiant smile, you haven't changed, Rosy dear, you are still my sweet golden doe. He can be romantic... He knows how to talk to women...

Look, Ernest and me, it's a long story... He was my teacher at Sydney School of Fine Arts. I instantly fell in love with him. He was so captivating, handsome, so athletic. He's put on a lot of weight since then, though he still has undeniable sex-appeal... He'd walk into the class, ascend the podium gracefully like a big cat. In winter, he even wore a fur coat. I tagged it his Oscar Wilde period, actually, he looked like Wilde with his grey eyes and lustrous, long hair. Both girls and boys stared in wonder. Next minute he would fumble through his papers, turn the projector on, get his long wooden ruler and point at every detail of the painting we were studying, its bold lines, the structure, the perspective. He'd go through Delacroix, Titian, Malevich, Kandinsky. Nothing deterred him. Sharp as a tack. He had a reputation for having affairs with his female students. I didn't tell any of my girlfriends, of course, but I wanted to sleep with him too. I'll have him, I said to myself. I was eighteen. He was in his late twenties, early thirties maybe. I was pretty, like any eighteen-year old. I just had to smile and men fell at my feet...

Anyhow, it wasn't very difficult to seduce him. One day I came to class in a low-cut top and leather mini-skirt. I had borrowed a pair of high-heeled boots from a girlfriend. I sat in the front row, right under his nose. After the lecture he called me over, asked if I liked Klee. I looked him in the eye and said he was my favourite painter. He smiled and said, come with me. He took my hand, led me down the corridor to a store-room, where we made love. He was such a brilliant lover... I had been with a few men... But none like him.

That day was the first time he called me his sweet golden doe. It could have just ended up as casual sex, but we stayed together for two years. And I'm sure he was faithful... Even if it's hard to believe... He was mad about my body... I was the first, yes, the first woman to sit for him. All those paintings from the Seventies, they're of me. He'd paint all day. In the evening, he was exhausted. Didn't matter... We had to make love. After each sitting, we had to make love... We couldn't help it. Him, looking at me. Me, looking at him. It was electric. And then I had to go back to Scotland for a while.

Yes, we were very much in love, but as soon I left he started seeing other girls. That's Ernest. You can't keep him on a leash. You just have to look at his work to understand that he worships the female body. What he paints is... very erotic. Yeah, he worships women. He would eat them if he could... But his art comes first, not the woman... I could never see him in a domestic relationship. That's why I was so surprised when I first heard that Lucie Bruyère had moved in to Longland... How did I hear about it? Through the grapevine. The Sydney art scene isn't that big and people gossip.

But Ernest is a loner. And, when he's working on a painting, he can't step a metre away from his easel. Ernest Renfield, his name will be remembered. His work has the touch of a genius. When you look at his nudes, it provokes a reaction, something deep, violent. He doesn't paint the flesh but tries to capture a vision... Did you see his retrospective in Canberra last year? All the nudes of the Seventies were there, those twelve portraits of me. I was intensely moved at seeing them again. And I remembered how he would gaze at me with a look that scared me. I had told him about it and he laughed away my fears: I'm not looking at you, Rosy dear, I'm looking *inside* you...

If it weren't for Ernest, I'd never be able to understand artists. They're a special kind, you know. Few can understand them. I can.

June Letourneau
Petersham
Sydney
New South Wales

Maman said I could stay downstairs for a while before going to bed. Someone at the party put a paper hat on my head. When they asked me to dance, Maman said, time to go to bed now. And we went upstairs to the bedroom. You know this bedroom, we've slept here before, Maman said. That time we saw a mother duck on the lake and her ducklings. I did remember the bedroom.

They were having fun downstairs. That wasn't fair. I wanted to stay at the party. But Maman said I was too young. She said children don't go to parties. When I'm older I'll go to parties. I put on my jammies and brushed my teeth.

It was cold in my bed. Maman said, it's time to go to sleep now. I asked her to tell me a story. She asked me what story I wanted to hear. I like the one about finding the golden stone in the river and asked her to tell it to me again. Maman told the story then said *bonne nuit*.

I didn't want her to close the door. I wanted to listen to the music. I couldn't sleep so I got out of bed and went to sit at the top of the stairs. From there you could see everything. I saw Maman talking with Ernest. He was dancing. He looks funny, that Ernest. He wants to paint my picture but Maman said, not until you're older, Ernest only paints grown-ups. I'd like to paint too but Ernest won't lend me his brushes. I'd like it if Ernest showed me how he paints but he says it's not for little girls.

After, I went back to the bedroom and stood at the window. That's when I saw the little girl on the lake. I put my hand over my face and looked through my fingers. But the little girl was still on the lake. I know who she is. She has written her name on the wall of the little house: SARAH. That's where she lives. That's where she goes to sleep at night. She's also written a number on the wall. It's 1-9-0-1. I remember that too.

Sarah saw me and she waved at me. And I waved back. She wanted me to go downstairs to play with her. Her face was all white, she was standing on the water. I stayed at the window to watch her. I told her in a secret language that I couldn't go outside to play because Maman said it was time to sleep. I heard a bird cry in a tree. Then I saw something else.

I saw Lucie... Yes, I know Lucie. She's always nice to me. She gives me cakes and cuddles me. She plays football with me when Maman is upstairs in the tower with Ernest. Maman gets painted in the tower. And Lucie was outside, she was going to the little house. I think she was going there because she wanted to say something to Sarah. There was someone else with Lucie. A man. He had a white beard... Yes, I saw him outside... No, I don't know him. He was talking with Lucie in the garden and he wasn't happy and she wasn't happy. The man ran after Lucie and grabbed her arm.

Sarah was in the little house. That's where she goes at night. The bird stopped crying. He was going to sleep. Everyone was going to sleep. Lucie had gone and the man with the white beard had gone. I went back to bed...

Yes, I know where Lucie was. She was on the path by the lake, down near the little house. Maman came upstairs and woke me up because it was time to go home. I put on my coat and my shoes and we went outside with Rosy.

Maman said she didn't like the lake. I could fall into the water. And when we walked down the path she said, be careful, it's dangerous, you could fall into the water and no one would know. And then Rosy said, I wonder why there are no lights around here, they should have spotlights. Rosy had a funny voice and walked funny too.

I saw something shiny in the grass, on the side

of the path to the little house... Yes, near the lake. Maman said, hurry up, sweetheart, get in the car, it's cold. But I ran to have a look at the shiny thing. Maman shouted, *arrête-toi*! I could tell she was angry. I stopped and said, but Maman, look, a golden stone, like in the story. Maman told me again that I could fall into the lake. She picked up the golden stone and screamed.

Rosy came and asked Maman what she had found. And the man also came to look at the stone and when he saw it he made an ugly face... Yes, it was the man with the white beard. I asked Maman why she had screamed. Then I asked if we had found the golden stone. And Maman said, no, it's not a golden stone, sweetheart. She was all white and the man said, as if he was going to cry: it's not a golden stone, it's Lucie's brooch.

Act III

Gary Whitehall
Australian Federal Police
Sydney Headquarters
New South Wales

I don't understand why I have been summoned... Yes, that's correct, I did leave Longland at three, as I indicated in my statement...

Pardon? You've been told that I spoke with Nicole and Rosy around four-thirty? What can I say? A glass of water? Yes please... I could be charged if I withhold information? Do you mind if I have a cigarette? Thank you... Listen, I would never want to mislead the police but the truth is I was scared for Lucie. I can't explain what was going through my mind last time we spoke. I wasn't thinking...

Between three and four-thirty? What did I do? I talked to Lucie. I thought it was an opportune time to have a serious talk about Ernest. No one knows him better than I do...

Pardon? What happened exactly? Ernest's argument with Sigotti stirred up bad memories. His behaviour was upsetting... It had me wanting to leave the party immediately. I grabbed my duffle-coat from the library and rushed outside. Yes, about three o'clock, as I explained last time... I just wanted to go home, go to bed and forget about the evening… As I strode across the terrace I heard someone moaning. I turned around and saw Lucie, sitting on the stairs, her face buried in her hands.

Yes, Officer, she did wear a tweed jacket… It was cold and windy… We were away from the guests. No, there was no one there other than us.

I thought Lucie may have been crying. I went to her and asked if everything was okay. She lifted her head, looked at me indignantly, and didn't answer. She wasn't crying. I mentioned Ernest's name and she snapped, mind your own business, you don't understand. I know what you think of him, Lucie went on, apropos of nothing. You think he's a hopeless drunk and a womanising ogre who'll spit me out tomorrow…

I said, what makes you think you're so different from the others? I've seen many women giving themselves up for Ernest's sake. I think you should be more cautious.

Lucie fired back… Ernest loves me as he's never loved anyone. No one understands him like I do, not even you, Gary.

I hope you're right, Lucie. But he's had many other meaningful relationships. He's had many grand passions before you. She went off the rails at that point, yelling, I don't want to hear your nasty lies about Ernest! Then she went on about how Ernest was wonderful, caring, how she could read him intimately, with her own heart...

The next moment, she sprung up and ran down the stairs. I followed her. She was a fair way away from me, running awkwardly in her high heels, running towards the lake. She stopped, turned to face me and went on about how little I knew of love, living alone in my Rose Bay apartment, surrounded by expensive works of art. She brought up the fact that I have lunch with my "mummy" every Sunday. True, my mother lives on the same street, two blocks away. She became quite malicious, going on about my mother missing out at being a grandmother, mummy's bad luck in my having no interest in women... Have you told mummy yet? she asked. Ernest isn't like you; he's not a fraud, a hypocrite. He doesn't lead a double life.

She was talking nonsense... She called me a fraud. I shook my head. It was pointless getting angry at her. What does she know about my life? I just wanted to give her a more complete picture of the Ernest I know...

Then she stepped in close to me. I could see she was trembling. Between clenched teeth, she snarled, what *exactly* do you want me to know about Ernest? Then she veered off and fled once more towards the lake. I implored her to stop because she had reached the marshes.

Soon after, she must have lost her footing because I lost sight of her. I moved closer to the edge of the bog. The moon cast its light on the surroundings, the shadows played tricks on me... I called out, but there was no answer. I took another step and that's when I heard her scream.

There she was... sunk to her waist. She had somehow managed to take her jacket off and her dress was torn. In desperation, she grasped at a clump of reeds. I came in closer and offered my hand, but she began to drift away, as if a current was dragging her out.

Her arms were flailing about and she was clearly panicking. She tried to haul herself up one more time by grabbing onto the reeds with both hands. She began to weep. There was nothing I could do but run back to the house and get help.

Just as I turned to go, she let go of the reeds. And the next minute, she was swimming across the lake. I cried out, Lucie, what are you doing? She was already half-way across and I doubt she could even hear me... Yes, Officer Lawson, she swam away... My head was spinning...

I staggered away from the mud, took the track that surrounds the lake, looking for Lucie in the water. I couldn't see her. Not knowing what to do next, I trudged back to the house.

I went up the stairs, across the terrace to the French doors, wide open to the night. I stood there for a while, bewildered and dizzy. The noise of the party was deafening. People were shrieking as they conga-danced all around the room, to that silly old song "Ça Plane pour Moi". There they were, stomping up and down the large staircase, and along the mezzanine, bellowing, "*Moi-moi! Moi-moi-moi!*"

I saw a long line of paper hats with coloured feathers over stoned, grinning, disfigured faces... masks, not faces... ghostly masks... floating, oblivious to my presence as I entered the room out of breath, dazed, drenched and dripping muddy water all over the floor.

Someone yelled, join in! A goatish-looking man let go of the woman in front of him, inviting me in. I turned away and looked for Ernest.

He was parading in the middle, performing some sort of wild dance. I went to him and took his hand to pull him away. He resisted and looked at me blankly. Without making a sound, I mouthed "Lucie". He poked his tongue out at me. I shouted that Lucie had gone into the lake. He shook his head and continued with his demented dance.

I went to the kitchen, where two adolescents sat, barely able to keep their eyes open. They were from Watooga, still in Year Twelve. They were the waiters for the party.

I was worried, Officer Lawson, I was worried about Lucie. But what else could I have done? I tried to tell Ernest she'd gone into the lake. I did what I could, Officer, believe me...

Ernest Renfield
Longland
New South Wales

I'd like to bring something to light, Lawson. It came to mind the other day, when was it, last Tuesday, when forensics searched the lake and found a human skull... By the way, anything new regarding that skull? You mean to tell me it has been sitting in the mud for nearly one hundred years? So, it all happened before my family bought the property...

Yes, my father's parents bought the estate in 1919. Do you reckon that could be the skull of an Aborigine? Hmm. We may never find out.

Talking about drowning, something has been bothering me since you told me that Lucie's brooch and shoes were found near the lake... Should we go to the sitting-room? You know the way, yes, to the right and down the corridor... After you, please. I want to be completely upfront with you. Would you mind closing the door, please, it's a very drafty house.

You might have heard that Lucie is a harmless little sprite who likes to play Bach and Mozart. I wouldn't dispute that, she has many good qualities, but she's also unbalanced... It's not easy to talk about it. Can you give me your word that my statement will never be used against her? Lucie is the sort of person to take her own life. Believe me… I'm so relieved that forensics haven't found her body in the lake. Just the same, I wouldn't have been surprised if they'd found her there.

Yes, jump off the cliff, hang herself, slit her wrists, swallow a box of sleeping pills, it's something she could very well do… I've been pondering her whole story, her past, her setbacks, her mother's death, her expectations since arriving here. I've had a growing concern that she could have turned her morbid melancholy against herself.

It's embarrassing, but let's be upfront. The first time you came here, I stated that Lucie and I had a few words regarding Rosy Barth on the Sunday morning. That's not exactly true. We didn't argue about Rosy. No, we didn't… It was already late in the day, we had missed lunch, the two waiters hadn't shown up and we were expecting our guests to arrive soon. We still had lots to do. The heavy couches and the chairs had to be moved, the rugs cleared, to make space for dancing. Lucie was giving me the silent treatment. God knows why, but she'd been sulking all morning. Then, out of the blue, she said she was sick and tired of putting up with my "issues". What on earth are you talking about, my dear, I asked. I know I can make a fool of myself when there's a good-looking girl flouncing about, but she was talking about something else altogether, my "drinking". First time she mentioned this since we've been living together. Then she asked me to keep my "consumption" under control, as she put it. Why would she confront me about this now, when we'd been living together for two years? What a perfect day to bring up a grievance like this! I told her we had more important matters to see to, like moving the couches. That made her angry. In fact, she was so infuriated that I thought she was about to hit me... That wasn't the first time either...

No, she's never hit me, but she can get terribly worked up. I've noticed how frustrated she gets when she can't express her thoughts accurately. She's an intelligent woman; her command of English is good, but she's always struggling with the subtleties. Anyhow, you'll understand my point in a minute...

Instead of giving me a hand with the couch, she went on strike. She sat down on a chair and declared that we had to discuss the matter. You are ridiculous, I told her. Why don't you make an appointment with a shrink? She was flustered now and asked me what in hell a shrink was. I sighed. So many things she's never heard of. I was going to explain when all of a sudden the two waiters turned up – two local kids I'd hired. Lucie dashed upstairs. I got the kids to help me shift the furniture...

Now, since last Tuesday I've been thinking of another incident, which took place in Paris last year. It had to do with Lucie's interviews with that violinist Jean someone... his last name eludes me. Lucie's old uncle had put us up. Since he lives in the country, the keys were with the concierge. Entering that pokey flat I realised that a cheap hotel room might have been a better option. The place was filthy and smelt of mould. Crikey, have you ever seen that black grime coating the walls, the windows? Nauseating. Lucie explained that these days her uncle barely used the apartment, and without a minute's delay, she set off to clean the dump. At least we were in a good location, ten minutes by foot from the Père Lachaise cemetery and five minutes to the nearest metro station...

I had a longing to go back to the Louvre. Yet going to the museum wasn't part of Lucie's schedule... When she wasn't busy interviewing her violinist, a couple of hours three times a week, she kept pestering me: let's go to the Galeries Lafayette! Let's go to Montmartre! What about paying a surprise visit to my friend Eric? You'll love his wife, Marianne! She's such a good cook!

I tried to explain: Lucie, I don't give a damn about your friend Eric and his wife. All I want to do is go back to the Louvre, can't you make an effort to understand that much? Well, she couldn't.

Anyway, we had argued so much, that evening I opted for the couch and let her keep the bed... So there I was, lying on this hard and narrow thing, wrapped in a smelly blanket, keeping one eye open, in case that crazy woman snuck up on me and stabbed me in the chest... I truly thought that our Parisian sojourn was going to end in a blood bath, and we'd make the front page of the tabloids. No, I'm not blowing it out of proportion... Anyhow, I managed to fall asleep shortly before dawn.

Now imagine, the first thing Lucie asked me that morning was how come I didn't sleep with her. You really are out of your mind, I said. Her eyes lit up with fury. She clenched her fists as if she was about to strike. Yes, I am serious... Abuse in relationships, you know, isn't always directed at women. Men cope abuse too. That's not uncommon... And when it comes to Lucie, aggression is always lurking beneath. There's a hidden perversity about her.

Oh no, I don't mince my words. Why should I? I've become aware of this troubling side of her. What I'd like you to know, Officer Lawson: Lucie, yes, Lucie Bruyère, isn't what she appears to be.

Don't believe what people tell you about her. Ask me, I've lived with her. You must live with people to know them. She's full of contradictions.

So, after two weeks of insufferable bickering, I told her I was going back to Australia. Your country, your family, driving hundreds of kilometres to see ugly churches, having to put up with uncouth French people blowing their cigarette smoke in my face, the traffic, the noise, the pollution, contemptuous waiters who pretend they don't speak English, restaurants serving raw meat and overcooked vegetables, I'm sick of it all, I announced. She begged me to stay. What about my family, she cried, what am I going to tell them?

She was in such a state that I told her, alright then, and I made the decision to stay. Go and see your friend Eric, while I go to the Louvre, I told her. We don't have to be in each other's pocket all of the time. I'll manage with a map. If I get lost, I'll ask a tourist, they are everywhere. But she got annoyed, it wasn't quite what she had in mind. That day, she had planned a few things for us, like a walk around the Palais Royal, where apparently Diderot and the Encyclopaedists used to hang out. She had booked a table at some trendy place in the Marais for lunch. We can be together for a change, she said, in Longland you spend so much time stuck in your tower, painting your life away. There are so many things I'd like to share with you... Then I snapped, shouting, painting my life away! Thank you very much! A nice way to put it! I told her I had more important matters to attend to than meeting up with the Encyclopaedists' ghosts. I have a rendezvous in the Louvre, I said, someone is waiting for me. She pressed me. Have you met someone? Who is she? She begged me not to leave her, then fell into one of her usual fits. But I'd had enough, in all honesty, it was excruciating.

Off I went. Finally alone. The day was radiant. I walked to the nearest metro station, alighted at Louvre Rivoli. I felt free at last. The terraces of the cafés were full of couples, who laughed, kissed and seemed to delight in some form of uninhibited sexual freedom that is typically French. Every time I smiled at one of those dolled-up women, I received a smile back. I strolled up the street and across the large esplanade of the Louvre. Yes, someone was waiting for me. It's a long story...

I fell in love with him many years ago. Ha, ha! Am I talking about a man? You sound surprised, Officer Lawson, and no, it's not a man. It's Gilles, the Pierrot painted by Watteau in 1719. I came upon the painting in an art book when I was thirteen. I spent hours contemplating this sad clown, with his shapeless body, and his vacant, moonstruck look, cramped in his silly attire, like me in my dreadful green school uniform. I had memorised each brushstroke of Watteau's work: the hat, the collar, the jacket with its row of big white buttons, the ruffles of the sleeves, the folds of the ankle-length white trousers, right down to the pinkish-red ribbons of his shoes. Gilles reminded me of the boy I was, a gigantic clown who didn't enjoy life while everyone around me was having a good time. A lonely lad and a figure of fun. I have gotten used to my giant frame over time, but I wasn't at peace with it in childhood. How could it be that my mother had given birth to such an odd colossus?

When my parents had gone to Watooga for an errand, I would slip into their bedroom to stand in front of the oblong mirror in the middle door of their oak wardrobe. Arms dangling to the side, I would hunch my back, let my body go slack, my shoulders, my stomach, my chin, imitating the village idiot. I'd become Gilles, the sad clown... Once, I even tried to dress up as Gilles. From my mother's chest of drawers, I borrowed one of her white nightgowns... I put on one of her petticoats, found an old straw hat from the garden rack and folded up the edges. I was Gilles!

That day, after the argument with Lucie, when I

saw him on the wall of the Louvre, I broke down... It took me back to that time, in front of the mirror in my parents' bedroom. Gilles, my twin, in his golden frame, in this faraway city, was looking at me with pity. I sat on the red bench and lost myself in rumination. Night had fallen. A museum guard tapped me on the shoulder. The Louvre was about to close.

I stood up mechanically and walked through the night, across the Seine, along the boulevards, down beside the quays... That was one of the most extraordinary nights of my life... The breeze was warm and smelt of sulphur, of damp soil, of the muddy scent of the Seine. I walked past grotty bars and brasseries, while the Eiffel Tower kept twinkling on. I was curious about the anonymous lives of these Parisians. I would have liked to follow someone, anyone, to their clandestine rendezvous. Where was the boat that would carry me away to Cythera? I was ready to embark. I felt so elated.

I walked for hours through Paris then returned to the musty smelling flat. Behind the door, what did I find? Lucie, on the floor, bawling her eyes out, a half-empty bottle of gin next to her. Where have you been, she screamed. I thought you'd run away, I was ready to call the police! That's always what she thinks I will do: leave her on her own.

But I said, as delicately as I could, there is nothing to worry about, I've been to my rendezvous. She mumbled, what rendezvous are you talking about? I answered the one with the boy, yes, a boy you have no reason to be jealous of. He will never leave his frame to interfere in your life, darling. His name is Gilles and Watteau painted him. Gilles, she said. Are you talking about a painting? Then she laughed like a lunatic and realised how foolish she'd been. I laughed uneasily in response.

I wish I could have held Lucie in my arms, but I couldn't. She was drunk, dishevelled, disfigured. I found her appalling. These three weeks in Paris were an eye-opener. I discovered a selfish and self-centred woman who required constant attention. I lack empathy for these people, I must confess. Sometimes I wish them a good deal of pain, yes, I wish them an illness, cancer. Lucie knew how important it was for me to visit the Louvre, an inspiring place, not that crummy Bordeaux museum with its pauper's art...

I hadn't been back to the Louvre in twenty years, and I realised how thirsty I had been for ideas, light, energy, colours, inspiration.

Our trip had been mapped out for Lucie's pleasure. Everything had to be done for her, in her own way, with no room for my interests. I have come to realise that Lucie is actually very different from the woman she presents to the world. Behind her assertive façade she's a vulnerable creature. If she's not looked after, she behaves like an insecure, whining little girl. One minute she's a kitten purring in your lap, the next, a vengeful harpy. What I wish to stress is that she's the sort of woman to take her own life. Yes, Officer Lawson, she is that depressive type... A lost soul. Believe me, no one really knows what's going on inside that pretty little head.

Jean Lucien
Faubourg Saint-Honoré
Paris
France

Thank you for coming to see me, gentlemen. It's very nice of you to spare some of your precious time. As I told Inspecteur Agnelli, I am not as mobile as I used to be.

Ahem... I beg your pardon? *Mon Dieu!* Twenty-four days already, that is concerning. I must admit I am distressed to hear you have no news on Mademoiselle Bruyère. I wish I could do something.

After Inspecteur Agnelli's last call, I decided to go through my diaries. At ninety-two, my memory is not always so reliable. Please take a look at what I've written here – that was when Mademoiselle Bruyère stayed in Beaux-de-Provence with her partner. Now remind me of his name, sorry, yes, that's it, Ernest Renfield...

There, under Saturday 17 and Sunday 18, that weekend, when they both came to my country house. As you can see I write everything down: what I eat, what I read, how much I've spent, and the people I meet and our conversations.

You might have heard that Monsieur Fargue

commissioned Mademoiselle Bruyère to write a book about my life... She interviewed me here, in this apartment, last year. We met each other ten times or so over three weeks. I got to know her a little bit better each week, and I was impressed by her musical insights and her appreciation of the composer Olivier Messiaen.

She sat there... in that chair. We talked with such ease that when the subject of the Stalag and my friendship with Messiaen came up, I had no qualms in discussing it. I was a notable violinist, but Olivier Messiaen, you see, was a genius...

We were incarcerated in Stalag VIII-A in Görlitz, in Silesian Germany... Ahem... Olivier was captured in Nancy in May 1940. I was caught a month later, in June, 20 June. I was transported to Silesia in a cattle truck... Stalag VIII-A was where Olivier wrote his capital piece, *Quartet for the End of Time*.

I see you are looking at my violin over there. I can't play it anymore; I have arthritis. Look at my left hand, these three fingers are as hard as steel. Old age robs you of everything... Anyway, you don't want to hear about my arthritis, but about Mademoiselle Bruyère.

Towards the end of our last interview, we were interrupted. It could have been around eleven o'clock in the morning when the bell rang. I opened the door; a strange looking fellow stood on the landing. He introduced himself as Mademoiselle Bruyère's partner. The man could not speak a word of French, though. As it happens, my English is not too bad. I had many opportunities to maintain my proficiency when touring America with the Orchestre de Paris after the war. We shook hands and exchanged greetings. Mademoiselle Bruyère immediately folded her notes, packed her tape-recorder and acknowledged him, though somewhat severely, I thought.

I realised I may not have the opportunity to meet Mademoiselle Bruyère again and suggested they join me in my country house in Beaux-de-Provence on the weekend. Mr Renfield instantly accepted. Mademoiselle Bruyère seemed unsure. She is such a genteel young woman. After a few seconds of consideration, she thanked me and said they would be delighted to come as long as it was not too exhausting for me... I assured them that my housekeeper would look after us well.

The following morning I packed a small bag and my niece Agnès drove me to Gare de Lyon. I caught the train to Marseille and later that afternoon was in Beaux, awaiting the arrival of my special guests. The weather was exceptional, we had refreshments by the swimming-pool. Mr Renfield told me he was a very well-known artist in Australia. I apologised for not having heard of him. I was sincerely embarrassed, but I must confess, I have little interest in contemporary art. He was certainly intelligent, and at that point I found him to be well mannered. After a time, his exuberance was wearying. I excused myself to have a rest before dinner...

Madame Martinet had made her succulent *tomates farcies* and a bouillabaisse. I opened two bottles of Saint-Emilion 1987. Mr Renfield seemed to enjoy the Saint-Emilion as he filled his own glass, to the brim...

Ahem... Madame Martinet waited at the table. She would normally have stayed the night in the room next to mine, but on this occasion she had to go home, as her children were visiting from Arles. This was badly timed. She has been a wonderful support to me since my wife died fifteen years ago. I like to have someone close-by at night time, especially since my heart problems started. Anyway, at the end of dinner I went upstairs to my bedroom. I lay in bed perplexed by Mr Renfield's behaviour, for while he had been chatty with me, he had not said one word to Mademoiselle Bruyère since their arrival at Beaux.

At around one o'clock a terrible commotion

woke me. Mademoiselle Bruyère let out a scream. That was her voice, without any doubt. I got up as quickly as I could, tottered up the corridor and stood quietly at their door. Not knowing if I should knock, I deemed it prudent to keep vigil. I sat down on one of the chairs on the landing and from there tried to hear what was going on. I heard Mademoiselle Bruyère sob, it went on for a while, then I heard her speak. They were having an argument about the rental car they had picked up at Marseille. It seemed that on the way out of the underground carpark, Mademoiselle Bruyère had scraped the passenger door against a pillar. Apparently Mr Renfield had refused to pay the excess on the insurance and they would be charged for the full cost of the repair.

Then in a low voice, she reproached Mr Renfield for constantly criticising her and watching her every move. Whatever she did was never right; he made her live in a state of constant anxiety, she said. Then her voice rose. You're not even talking to me, she shouted, but you had no problem chatting up that waitress. How long before you dare utter a word to me? There was no answer from Mr Renfield, no reaction. I could make out his heavy steps pacing the room.

After a while Mademoiselle Bruyère's voice broke

the silence again… You are never happy! We rent a car, it's not comfortable enough for you. We travel by train, it's too noisy for you. We had the use of a flat in Paris, but it was too dirty for you. Your trip to the Louvre, coming back home at the crack of dawn when the museum closes at six. I was worried sick about you! And then I end up scraping the door of the car because I'm a mess. I live under the sword of Damocles. I never know when it's going to fall.

Then I heard a muffled noise, like someone slumping onto the floor. Look at me, Mademoiselle Bruyère said in a pathetic voice. Look what you've done to me. Mr Renfield was still pacing the room. Another long silence, before she continued… I had in mind that you would like this trip, I could show you my country. But I should have come by myself. You're only happy in Longland, in your tower, with your painting.

Then came a cold, superior voice, hissing, you are a weak person, Lucie Bruyère, and I have no time for weak people. Look at you, lying on the ground, are you mad? Now, please, would you be kind enough to get up from the floor, go perform your ablutions and let me get to bed?

You've ignored me all the way from Marseille, she replied. I don't understand what's going on. Why do you hurt me? You don't hurt people when you love them.

After a few seconds I heard his detached voice... I hurt you because something in you allows me to do so. You allow yourself to be hurt...

Listening to that man I grew rather upset. How could he speak so disparagingly to a woman? I could hardly imagine what wrong she had done to be treated like this. I thought that she needed to take a stand.

Some minutes passed, without her saying anything. I imagined her shocked, lying on the cold tiles. I heard her weeping. After a while, the bed creaked and within minutes Mr Renfield was snoring. Mademoiselle Bruyère continued to weep. After what seemed a very long time, I heard her shuffle off the floor and get into bed. I went back to my bedroom... Ahem... I was too dismayed to go to sleep and so sat at my desk to record in my diary this disturbing episode.

The following morning, I was awoken by the slamming of car doors. I looked out the window and Mademoiselle Bruyère and Mr Renfield were in their vehicle, ready to leave. They had not even said goodbye or offered a thank you. By the time I got downstairs, the engine was running, with Mr Renfield behind the wheel. He looked at me vacantly. I approached the car. Mademoiselle Bruyère wound down her window. She had tears in her eyes. She looked fatigued and miserable. She presented her hand to me and I held it tenderly. She thanked me for my candour during our interviews and for the hospitality. Mr Renfield told her to hurry up. The automatic window began to rise at his bidding and Mademoiselle Bruyère quickly withdrew her hand.

I've suffered greatly in my life. I've seen what people can do to one other. In my experience, there are those who don't hurt others, or at least try their best not to, and if they do, unintentionally, they know it in their hearts and they are remorseful. And then there are those who hurt others, without the slightest compunction. They hurt others in thought, word and deed and snore through the night completely unperturbed.

Sylvia Normand
Missing Person Department
Poitiers
France

Look, I already know what you're going to tell me... I know I should have contacted you three weeks ago, when you called my sister Mathilde. You see, Inspecteur Agnelli, I didn't want to upset my husband. But never mind, he can go to hell... I've been feeling so guilty not telling you about the phone call... Yes, I got a call from my sister Lucie on the Sunday she went missing.

We were having lunch with my two sons. I'd set the table on the veranda. The phone is in my husband's office at the back of the house. It must have been about five o'clock, we were having coffee... I left the table to take the call. It was Lucie, she was crying. At first, I couldn't make sense of what she was trying to tell me. After a while she settled down and muttered, Sylvia, I need help.

I should have been in touch with you three weeks ago, I know. I feel terrible about it... It's my husband, you see, he keeps saying, if your sister calls just hang up, always something wrong with that woman...

Lucie was sobbing. I could hear that "Macarena"

song in the background. People were laughing and shouting. Lucie finally managed to explain, Sylvia, things aren't going so good over here, I shouldn't have left. Is it Ernest? I asked. My life is in danger, she whispered. I tried to play it down... What danger are you talking about, I'm sure it's not as serious as you think... The truth is that I didn't know how to deal with it. My sister and I, we've never been that close. She doesn't confide easily in others.

Five minutes into the conversation I heard my husband yell out: who's calling, on a Sunday afternoon? I started to get annoyed. Lucie's such a drama queen. And what can I do, honestly? She lives on the other side of the world. If only she'd moved to Spain or Italy, I could have jumped on a train and tried to help, but I wasn't going to jump on a plane to Australia. A plane to Australia! That's grounds for divorce.

Well, I said to her, you must come back to France. She didn't say a word. Then she began wailing... How do you expect me to come back when I have no money? I didn't comment. Let me tell you, I'm truly ashamed of what went through my mind, but I thought, you've got some nerve! You make a big fuss telling me your life is in danger, why not be upfront and ask for money? I could hear my husband shouting, Sylvia, tell them to go to hell! Your sons came all the way from Angoulême to spend the day with you! I was so stuck in my own views and upset by my husband's yelling that I simply repeated, Lucie, you must come back to France. She started crying again. Look, Sylvia, she said after she'd collected herself, do you understand what I'm telling you? And she repeated loudly, each word like a drumbeat: I HAVE NO MONEY. She explained how four weeks in France last year had cost the earth. She had to pay excess on the rental car, using up all of her savings. I'm broke, she cried. You get it? I have no money. How can I come back? I didn't know what to say and flew off the handle at her, shouting, why don't you ask Mathilde? She's rich. I immediately regretted what I said. It was cruel. Cruel and stupid. I waited for her to hang up. I know too well that my sister Mathilde and her husband wouldn't lift a finger for Lucie. They don't help anyone but themselves. They're stingy.

Anyway, I can't blame anyone but myself. Money? I could have lent her money... I could have given her some money... I work full-time. I'm a high school teacher. So is my husband. I'm not that rich, but I have some money put aside... I didn't offer any help. I feel terrible. I feel terribly guilty... Goodness, I could have given her enough for the plane ticket. The flight isn't cheap, but how much is a life worth, especially the life of your own sister?

We endured a long silence. I could still hear the "Macarena" song. It was so irritating. I didn't even ask Lucie why her life was in danger. I didn't want to know. I just wanted to put an end to our phone call, hang up, go back to the veranda, finish my coffee, give a hug to my daughter-in-law who's six-months pregnant. Then Lucie, in a cold voice, said, your happy little life has turned you into a selfish person, Sylvia.

I was so upset by her words. I should have never said what I said next, but I couldn't help myself: I don't get you Lucie, what you're telling me is so confusing, I don't understand a word of your story. What exactly do you want from me? She countered scornfully, saying, yes, that's right, you don't understand. Well, it's true that in many ways I didn't understand because I didn't want to understand. Lucie, she challenges you, she doesn't give you any respite, and I don't like it. It makes me feel uncomfortable.

Neither of us said anything for a while. My husband had stopped calling out to me. Lucie, are you still there? I asked quietly after some time. What are you afraid of? Talk to me. Shouldn't you call the police? In a flash she answered: look, forget about it, it's not worth it, I'll let you go now. What time is it in France? Five o'clock. It's three here... No, three in the morning... The music, yes, we're having a party... Oh, sorry, you haven't finished your lunch. I know you like to take your time. Sorry for being such a nuisance... Give my regards to your family. Her voice was sad.

I repeated without conviction, you must find a way to come home. Can't you find a job over there? You've got a degree, it should be easy for you. Then she replied, that's a good idea, Sylvia, I'll look for a job. Bye now... And she hung up. I returned to the veranda. I felt like I'd let Lucie down. My husband asked what the phone call was about. I said it was just one of the neighbours waffling on. I couldn't finish my coffee. It had gone cold. I just hope it wasn't your sister, my husband said. He isn't a bad man. But he doesn't have much time for people like Lucie, people who aren't like him, without children and a regular income... Lucie ran away from home when she was underage, yes, she was seventeen back then, and he's always thought she wasn't a good example for our two children. You know how teenagers are so easily influenced. And yes, my parents had to report her as a missing person. Everyone was very worried... But that was ages ago. Twenty-five years ago. Lucie has changed since then...

As I was gazing at the red and white napkin I wondered if Lucie hadn't spoken the truth. My tongue was like a piece of dry leather in my mouth. She said I'd turned into a selfish person. I looked at my children... My youngest son was planning a trip to China. He's twenty-six. He'd never been overseas before. Would it be better to go through Dubai or Moscow? Moscow was a beautiful city worth a visit. What do you think, mum? I didn't answer. Do you become selfish when you've got all that you need? We bought our house on a twenty-year mortgage. It's paid off now. We've never had major health issues. Our children are good kids.

As I was about to leave the table my husband caught my vacant look and said, next time your sister calls, I'll talk to her myself. We don't want anything to do with her, is that clear? I said, yes, next time you can talk to her.

As a matter of fact, I didn't want to think about Lucie anymore. My husband was right. She was too much trouble. If she needed money, she'd better look for a job. That shouldn't be so hard. Things are easier down there. It's supposed to be paradise... My Goodness, how heartless! Now I feel terrible...

This mess, you see, this mess wouldn't have happened if it weren't for my mother. Why? She pushed her to leave... Each time Lucie didn't feel right about going to Australia, our mother urged her to go. It was always push, push, push. You've found the man of a lifetime, she badgered. He's wealthy. He'll provide for all your needs. You won't have to worry anymore. You won't have to work. Look at me, the tax department has raided everything. I have breast cancer. If I'm lucky I might live another two months. Go! Don't hang around. He's asked you to move in with him... Get going before he changes his mind. I told my mother so many times to stop haranguing her.

The whole thing was kind of too good to be true. I had a strange feeling. I didn't think Lucie had thought things through. What did we know about Ernest Renfield? Nothing. And my mother thought Lucie had found Mr Right. How could I guess what was going to happen? Who knows where Lucie is? Who knows if she's still alive? It's such a terrible thing to have done. To your own sister... I feel awful. What if he's keeping her locked up somewhere? What if she's been murdered? It's my little sister, for heaven's sake. She's far away, on her own. And that man... I've seen him... There's something funny about him... Who knows what he's capable of. He could be a serial killer. They look like normal people, you know... You've seen them in your job, haven't you? They could be your next-door neighbours. You've got to be careful, especially in a foreign country. If something serious has happened, I'll never get over it.

Act IV

Ernest Renfield
Longland
New South Wales

Now please, Officer Lawson, can you ask your men to leave my studio? Why are you tormenting me? Your search warrant won't bring you any closer to the truth. You and your men are wasting your time here...

You think I've killed the poor sod and dumped her body in the forest? Think I'm a nutcase and a rapist? But I haven't done anything, I'm not a murderer. Someone's told you that I'm unhinged... Or would you prefer to tick another box, such as deranged... depraved... manic... sicko... pervert?

You smashed the door of my studio and violated my sacred space. This is the reward for my honesty and hospitality? You took the liberty of looking at my paintings without my consent, when they were not meant to be seen. That's abuse of power! What sort of a man are you, Lawson? How would my paintings have anything to do with Lucie's disappearance? It's preposterous! And as for this bloody search warrant, you ought to know that having strangers hanging around gets on my nerves... Thank you, gentlemen...

Should I follow you to the police station for interrogation? Will your judicial tribunal condemn me for what I've painted? I haven't got blood on my hands... Thanks for your concern, my head is alright, it's just a small cut. Your brutes didn't muck around, did they? Look at the mess they've made in here.

How dare you question my sanity? Oh, I can see on your face that you believe I'm mad. Because of what you have seen here. My work repulses you.

Why did I paint these pictures? Good question. It's only fair that you ask, Lawson. Remember the parable of the tight-rope walker? Well, I am a funambulist and every day I cautiously start on that rope, pulled taut. I get half-way across, an unforgiving wind catches me unprepared, and my head spins, my legs shake. And that jester appears; he shouts, laughs, teases me; he knows how weak I am, how pathetic I've always been and like a crow about to pick out someone's eyes, he goes, nark, nark, nark. Then he yells, you ought to be locked up, Renfield, you ought to be locked up! And every day I fall, crashing to the ground. Without painting, Lawson, without my studio, I *would* go insane.

Each morning I wake up with a blissful heart, ready to forgive my good old friends who once upon a time loved me... They would have done anything for me. I thought they would have gone up the holy stairs of the Scala Sancta on their knees for me. One can be so naïve when it comes to being loved... When your market value plummets, when the circus is about to leave town, when the bear is too old for the show, your good brothers and sisters do a runner.

I'll have been dead for years and yet my work will prevail. All my cockroach friends will be dead, buried and forgotten. The art dealers will be forgotten too. Who out of Picasso and Kahnweiler do we remember? No one even knows what Kahnweiler looked like. My courtiers loved me once, but they took their love back as if retrieving a cheap watch from a pawn broker. By the end of the day, I am a sad clown, desolate and bereft...

These days I stand before my easel with the best of intentions. I should see, sitting here, young Emma, or Kate, or Julia, the shop assistant from Watooga Fruit and Veg, as some hieratic Goddess who presides over us. I should see Emma, Kate or Julia as essential beings rather than physical ones. A god somewhere, after all, has given the artist the task of making perfect what he could not.

But when I look at them, I can't resist the evil pull. I turn beauty into abjection, for to me the girls smell of death. See in this one, Lawson, Emma looks like a dead fish. And look, if I turn the painting upside down, she looks like a set of rotten teeth.

People, especially women, think I worship women. Ask them! I declared many times in television interviews that the "second sex" is more honest, more gifted and more sensible than men. I'll tell you in confidence, Lawson, I never believed a word of it... I need girls to pose for me. They are the raw material of my work. Women's curves sell better. But like most men, I never looked at women as more gifted and more sensible. Come on, women, I love them young, good-looking and silent. Yes, I'm typical of so many men of my generation, and I'm not ashamed of it. Women's beauty has always fascinated me, as a painter and a man, yet by the same token I've always feared it. Emma is like a venomous flower, enticing you before trying to swallow you whole.

The *vagina dentata*, ever heard of it? The vagina is like a toothed hole, well, like a spiked pit trap in the jungle, if you prefer. That's what women are... What about this one, here in the corner? Do you recognise her? It's Nicole, our dear old Nicole with her saggy tits and her fat thighs, her dried up, deterring cunt. And over there... Look at that one. Don't move, I'll bring it closer to you. Do you recognise her? It's Lucie, yes, that's her! Charming on the outside, but inside a pack of lies, lies I could see after I'd cut her open...

I have no illusions regarding mankind. You, for instance, Lawson, if I had to paint a portrait of you, any idea of what it'd look like? Messed up? Repulsive? Four of your men forced their way into my studio... Yes, indeed, with an axe, if you please... Is that fair play? Do you understand me any better now that you've pulverised my door and violated my works? No, you don't.

I sent a hundred and twenty printed invitations in immaculate white envelopes for that fucking party. Cost me a fortune in printing, drinks, food, flowers. You've seen the list of guests, haven't you? I invited my brothers and sisters openheartedly. Do you know how many of my good old pals came along? Well, fifty-seven... Fifty-seven turned up. And sixty-three did not.

After my New York exhibition, my place would have been too small to welcome all my brothers and sisters. But today, I'm not good enough. That's what the life of an artist is: he becomes a ghost before his own death... Renfield? You mean Renfield, the painter? Is he still alive? I thought he died years ago. Oh well, we haven't heard much from him lately. You think he's still painting? Can you hear them? Well, I can.

Lucie has messed up my life. She never says anything. She never complains about anything. She takes it all in without protest then stares you out with her teary eyes. She feels sorry for me like some Sister of Mercy… By the way, did you know that Domenico Veneziano painted the martyrdom of Saint Lucie? Saint Lucie is silenced by the soldier with a dagger to her throat, blinded when her eyes are gouged out… Lucie who sees everything, who wants to save me from myself, who wants to love me but doesn't know how, who wants to give her life up for me without knowing the meaning of martyrdom.

"Women, inspire us with the desire to do masterpieces, and always prevent us from carrying them out." Isn't that true? You know who wrote that? Oscar Wilde. Lucie inspired me to start with, oh yes, she was so pure and fresh, I loved that girl when she rang from the other side of the world. That sweet voice gave me a hard on. Loved that girl when she slipped her little hand down my groin to unzip my pants, calling me her fat bunny rabbit, her old fat bunny rabbit, while giving me a blow-job. She made me forget my age, my old creaky bones, my painful joints. Be gone, pot-belly! It was as if I had found myself in the time machine and become Rod Taylor, younger, stronger, a fucking stud. I was forty again, like her, at the beginning of life, when you still have time to waste.

Loved her when she made me think I could start again from scratch, and all my fuckups and lies would be forgotten, forgiven, wiped out. Loved her when she said I was going to paint again, that time had no value, how the greatest artists reach their peak late in life. Loved her when she said she was going to give me a special kind of love, she was going to teach me baby steps in the art of loving, that age didn't matter, when she said that my old age wasn't a threat because she couldn't see my spots, my warts and my furrows, because she only saw my smile, my cheeky smile, she said, and my jokes, she said, made her laugh. I loved her because I believed her.

I was under her spell but then the demons caught up with me. See, that woman turned out to be a pain in the arse. I'll tell you what, Lawson, I will paint my ultimate work. See, what you're looking at now is rubbish, it stinks, it's rat shit. It was not my hand moving the brush, it was someone else's hand, someone who'd snuck into my studio. I didn't paint that picture! From now on, I'll keep well away from these dark visions, fix my gaze on the sublime blue sky. I haven't got much time left but I'll come back as the leading light of the post-modern avant-garde...

Come closer, Officer Lawson, I'd like to show you a real beauty, a piece of art, that is sure to perk you up. Look, over here, on the wall, see the red velvet curtains. Look carefully now, I'm going to open them just for you... I see you recognise the painting. I knew you had the true soul of an artist... Yes, *L'Origine du Monde*, a wonder, isn't it? Gustave Courbet painted it and I have reproduced it. Back in 1988, I was in New York, at the Courbet retrospective in Brooklyn. The masterpiece was there, a great bushy pubis revealing a young and inviting vagina. I knew the curator and he let me in after-hours so I could be with my nude. Over many nights, I set my easel six feet away from Courbet's work and endeavoured to reproduce it. I gave it my best shot. It's now my consolation prize...

I'm sure Courbet truly worshipped women. I might not love them enough, who knows? I can't imagine my parents fornicating sixty-three years ago to conceive me. Knowing that I came out of that place, well, it's upsetting.

But I must move on, make an effort to complete my definitive work. It will take time and I'll have to find the right model. Silly Lucie promised she would be my last muse. It didn't work, Lawson, she's tense, prissy and too intellectual. I can't stand women who are always questioning what I do.

When my last painting is done, I'll be at peace. And I'll go quietly, like a tiny bird, a fairy wren, fschuuut... Like friar Brett Whiteley, see, what a final adventure! Just like him, I'll book a room in a motel, an ugly-looking red brick dump on the side of a busy road, and then lights out, gone!

What now, Lawson? Are you taking me? You'll handcuff me and I'll get taken away like a lunatic, a criminal, a convict, on a cart pulled by a skeletal horse. Past the hateful crowd and then up onto the scaffold. To be one of Goya's ghosts... You're leaving? Already? Is that it? No scaffold yet, Officer Lawson? See you next time then. I won't leave town, I promise. I won't leave this house, I won't even leave my tower. Where would I go?

Nicole Letourneau
Australian Federal Police
Sydney Headquarters
New South Wales

Sorry, I don't understand... I'm not familiar with the Australian criminal justice system... I could be charged? Along with Mrs Barth and Mr Goszyński? Who is Mr Goszyński? Oh Gary, so that's his name... Charged for withholding crucial information? But why? What information? You want me to read this statement? Okay.

"*Australian Federal Police. Canberra. Case R/B 17630-360.* Mrs Virginia Hackton, (38) bank clerk in Canberra, declared that on 30 October 2000 she stayed the night at Mr Ernest Renfield's house, 220 Longland Road, in Longland. Mrs Hackton was woken up around 5.00 a.m. by the sound of gunshots, leaving her bedroom immediately thereafter. Mrs Hackton declares that Mr Renfield's bedroom door was ajar and that Mrs Nicole Letourneau, (39) shop assistant in Sydney; Mrs Rose Barth, (50) art dealer in Sydney; Mr Gavril Goszyński, (65) art dealer in Sydney, were standing inside. *Statement recorded on 20 November 2000 by Officer Samuel Douglas.*"

I don't know what to say... Mr Pietro Negri's

statement corroborates Mrs Hackton's... Really? Do you mean that I might go to jail? But I am a single parent, with a little girl to look after. I haven't done anything wrong, Officer Lawson.

What time was it when I picked up the brooch? Four-thirty... How can I be so sure? I looked at my watch, with the full moon above, there was definitely enough light to see the time. I was worried about June being so close to the lake. It was really a stupid idea to have brought her along...

Anyway, as we were approaching the car, Gary appeared. He was squeezing something under his arm. As he got closer to us, I figured it was a tweed jacket. What are you doing with Lucie's jacket? I asked. I found it there, he muttered, pointing towards the lake. Suddenly June cried out, look Maman, here she is, here she is again. Gary went berserk. He looked over towards the far bank of the lake and asked whom June was talking about. Have you seen someone over there? I asked. Yes, I just saw her, replied June, here she is again. Gary seemed to now be in quite a state of agitation. I tried to keep hold of my daughter but she'd started running towards the lake.

She's obsessed with a little girl, I explained. Every time we come here, she drives us crazy with stories about a little girl. June had got to the caretaker's house and called out, she's in here! As she walked to the door, she said, Sarah, why don't you want to talk to me? The big fig tree above the old caretaker's house kept everything dark. Rosy was very drunk but she remembered there was a miniature torch in her handbag.

As we got to the abandoned caretaker's house, I heard a noise, as if someone was crying inside. I thought it might be Lucie seeking refuge. Why? Well, um... Lucie wanted to leave Longland... She wanted to leave Ernest. Yes, I should have told you in the first place, but I promised Lucie that I wouldn't tell a soul. She called me on the Friday prior to the party, told me she wanted out, she had plans to flee.

Why did she want to leave Ernest? She said she could no longer put up with his behaviour... I'd better leave now, she said, otherwise if he doesn't kill me, I'm going to kill him... When I sat for Ernest he told me how Lucie often got hysterical. He was worried for her. He asked me if I knew a good psychoanalyst in town, preferably French-speaking.

As I'm telling you all of this, it sounds as though Ernest is all sweet. But there is another side to him. I've seen Ernest out of his wits and believe me, he can be terrifying. Forget that argument he had during the party with the guy in the white tuxedo, that was a trifle. What I've seen is much scarier... Like that Sunday, when Lucie and June were playing football and little June broke a terracotta pot. Nothing exceptional, just a small lemon tree in a pot... It tumbled down the stairs... Ernest heard the noise. He left his brushes, ran to the garden and went completely insane. He railed, especially at my daughter, and I could see Lucie was petrified. His face was scarlet. I tried to calm him down but he let fly at me too. The three of us then endured a relentless barrage of vicious comments about how careless and selfish we were. Even with June in tears he showed no restraint. Eventually he turned around and disappeared for the rest of the day.

Anyway, as we reached the caretaker's house, I asked if there was anyone there. It's me, Nicole, I said. No one answered. Rosy pushed the door open. She walked in first, flashing her torch around the room. A few yellowing papers and an old plastic pen were lying on a wooden table that had been pushed against the window. Lucie must have forgotten them the previous summer when she worked on her biography of Jean Lucien. Even though the caretaker's house has few comforts, it has always given her a peaceful working environment, away from Ernest.

We searched the house, including a broom cupboard tall enough for an adult to stand in, but there was no one in sight. We could still hear a kind of wailing nearby. Eventually we began to walk out, Rosy leading with her torch. Shush, she said, it's coming from over there. We stopped moving. We were dead silent, standing there for an eternity. After a while the sounds of the night returned and we made a move.

June clung to me as we trudged back up the path. As Rosy was rummaging for her car keys to return the mini-torch to its clip, she began shrieking that her wallet was missing. She complained about having bought a cheap, nasty handbag, saying that it might have fallen out, as the zipper was defective. She began to walk back to the main house to search for her wallet.

I said, you go and we'll wait for you here. Gary didn't say a word. His teeth were chattering and he looked drained. June was about to collapse from exhaustion. After what seemed like a long while I suggested to Gary we go and look for Rosy. That's when we heard the two explosions. Like two blasts... No, I'm not able to tell where they came from. They could have come from the main house or the forest. Sounds get swept down the creek and always seem closer than they really are... Gary threw his hands up. He looked terrified. I took June in my arms. We ran up to the main house.

On the terrace, the glass doors had been left wide open. We walked inside. The reception room was bedlam. It looked as if the place had been ransacked. The floor was littered with confetti, plastic cups, dirty plates, tissues, napkins, empty bottles. Layers of pink streamers covered most of the furniture, though I could make out the red wine stains on the expensive white leather couch.

Well, it had been a wild party; people had been drinking heavily and doing drugs... I cleared the couch and laid down little June, who had fallen asleep in a chair. We called out to Lucie. We called out to Ernest. Nothing. Then Rosy appeared in the doorway, pallid, with her mouth agape, clearly distressed. Her right hand was bloody. She also had blood on her lips. Registering the alarm on my face, she replied that she had cut herself on a piece of broken glass. I asked where Ernest was and she mumbled that we should look upstairs.

I led the way, with Gary and Rosy close behind as we crept up the stairs. Gary was the one who knocked at Ernest's bedroom door. We waited a few moments before entering the room. We tiptoed towards the bed. The odour was heavy and sickening: a mix of musty bed linen, the reek of spilt liquor, stale sweat oddly overlaid with the smell of patchouli oil...

Ernest likes collecting antiques... you've seen his house... but his bedroom is without doubt the most over the top. It's like a bazaar, decked out in Indian red, velvet drapes around the bed, cluttered with statues, chandeliers, artefacts, Moroccan brass lamps, wall hangings... But the centrepiece is the huge, canopied four-poster bed... You could almost imagine it being custom-made for Ernest.

He was there, yes, Ernest, in his gigantic bed; right in the middle, on his back, his arms outstretched. His pyjama top was unbuttoned, the sheet pulled up to his waist. He was asleep. His face was red and swollen, his grey hair sticking out. The day was dawning; the soft light caught the Saint-like figures of the bed's bas-relief. The drapes hung from the canopy like cataracts of blood, framing the bulk of Ernest's body... A surreal vision.

Rosy and I drew closer to each other. Gary called to Ernest. There was no reaction, so he checked to see if he was still breathing. He tapped him on the shoulder. Ernest didn't budge. He was absolutely still. Gary looked at us and whispered that he must have drunk too much and passed out. He could have taken pills as well. I've never known anyone able to sleep so soundly with three people hovering over them. It did cross my mind that he wasn't asleep...

The guests who were staying overnight had been woken up by the two blasts and were now standing on the mezzanine. I could hear snatches of their alarmed murmurs... Gary lifted a finger to his mouth, beckoning us not to make a sound. Then he walked out of the bedroom and explained to those on the mezzanine that the noise most likely was from hunters shooting deer. This was hunting season, he said, and dawn is the best time to catch a deer.

They seemed satisfied and returned to their rooms. I suggested we go back to the sitting-room. I wanted to check if Lucie's travelling bag was still there. You see, when Lucie called me on Friday, she had planned to hide a small travelling bag somewhere in the house. Initially, she thought about leaving her stuff outside but I advised her that inside would be more practical. That way, she could discreetly immerse herself among the departing guests and make her way to the car.

I assumed that she wanted to leave specifically on the night of the party because she would be able to get a lift out of Longland. I also advised her to leave all of her manuscripts behind. This upset her, but as I explained, this was the best way not to rouse any immediate suspicions from Ernest. She promised that she would.

Now, I had no idea that June and I would be coming to the party in Rosy's car. That Saturday morning, my old bomb refused to start. I called Rosy just in time to get a lift to Longland. Lucie saw us arrive in a car that was not mine and when she figured I had travelled with Rosy, she pulled me aside and curtly said, I am not going anywhere with that woman. She didn't trust Rosy and was convinced she would jeopardise her plans to leave Ernest.

We left the bedroom. I walked downstairs, followed by Rosy and Gary. I entered the sitting-room and tried to find Lucie's bag… It was nowhere to be seen. I assumed that Lucie had taken it. Rosy asked me what I was looking for. I'm looking for your wallet, I lied. Didn't you say that you lost your wallet around here? Rosy scoffed and said, no, no way, and that her handbag had been in the library.

We headed to the library. We searched but couldn't find the wallet, Rosy groaning every now and then that she had three hundred dollars in there. Her state of anxiety seemed out of proportion to what had been going on.

I didn't know where Lucie was and was too exasperated to hang about any longer. I suggested to Rosy we leave without the wallet and I offered to drive. Gary carried June to the car.

No, believe me, I don't know where Lucie is. She hasn't contacted me. I swear, Officer Lawson, she hasn't called... I can't imagine what could have happened to her. I know she was fearful of Ernest's reaction... No woman would want to stand up to that man when he's angry...

I didn't call the police until the following Wednesday as I thought it would give her at least three days to hide... Yes, that's right, eventually I did call the police even though I had pledged secrecy to Lucie because I had grown worried, very worried...

Wait, I just remembered something else... When we were in the caretaker's house, I picked up a piece of paper lying on the table. I recognised Lucie's handwriting. I took it with me. One of Lucie's poems. I brought it along to show you.

The one who has been broken
Blinded by pain
Seeks in a lover whom he doesn't see
Another lover who will never be
His heart begs for love
Yet love is nowhere to be seen
For whom has been broken
By pain.

Gary Whitehall
Paddington
Sydney
New South Wales

I remember Virginia Hackton rather well. She was standing on the mezzanine with the other guests who were staying the night at Longland. From her statement, I can see she would make a very good detective indeed.

Yes, I was in Ernest's bedroom. I admit to lying and withholding information. And yes, I confess that I lied; I would do it again if I had to. I did it for Ernest. Because he's my dearest friend, he's the younger brother I've never had and I feel a duty to protect him... Yes, to protect him.

You see, that night, when Nicole, June and I were in the former caretaker's house, when we heard the sound of gunshots, I remembered all of a sudden that Ernest kept a hunting-gun in his sitting-room. It belonged to his grandfather. They used to go hunting together... No, I wouldn't be able to give you more details about it. I'm not an expert in firearms. When I heard the two blasts, I initially thought that Ernest might have done something terrible... gone too far...

Perhaps I should start at the beginning. There's

something about Ernest's past that you should know. I had hoped that he would be seen solely as a great artist, without the burden of his disturbing past. But I've come to realise that it's impossible.

Twice in his life Ernest has been admitted to a mental hospital. The first internment occurred when he was thirty. Back then we shared an apartment in Kings Cross. A night patrol found him wandering about the city centre almost naked. The policemen assumed he had been in a fight, seeing he was bruised and bloodied. When asked who he was, he answered, I am Diogenes. When asked his address, he said, I live inside a barrel in Martin Place and intend to be a living example of virtue. They drove him to the St Vincent's Hospital Psychiatric Unit. To the nurses and psychiatric staff who tried to work out his identity, he kept on affirming that he was Diogenes. Every morning, they'd find him asleep on the linoleum floor. Four days later, the police finally identified him and called me – Ernest and I had been living together for about two years. That episode happened shortly after his big show in New York. Fame hadn't done him any good.

A few weeks prior to that incident, I was witness to Ernest's deepening madness. I had just opened the gallery and business was sluggish. One afternoon, I came home early. Ernest was talking loudly. He was in his room and I thought he had someone with him. His door was ajar and I peered in. He was on his own and raving. I couldn't understand his mumbo-jumbo, and then, suddenly, he let out a long scream. Then he started throwing around his paint pots, his brushes, ripping up canvasses, before flinging his easel against the wall. I was shocked by this outburst. The next minute I heard him wailing before he snapped. Fuck it all, fuck everything, leave me alone, I've had enough, he screamed.

I left the apartment, found myself heading in the direction of Centennial Park. I don't know how many circuits of the park I did before I found the courage to return home... I walked in. I called out to Ernest. He came forth to greet me, in his customary jovial way, as if nothing had happened. I have never told anyone about that episode.

I remember back then the psychiatrist had diagnosed Ernest with schizophrenia. I'm not a world expert on mental illness, but I believe that these days he would more likely be told he was suffering from Narcissistic Personality Disorder. Anyway, the psychiatrist prescribed him tablets, which eventually must have worked, as three weeks later he came home.

Yes, he stayed three weeks in that psychiatric

unit. He had aged and lost weight. That was heart-breaking... Then we got organised. A friend partitioned the largest room into two. One would become Ernest's studio and the other his sleeping alcove, with a small fold-up bed and a sink. We screwed a strong bolt on the outside of the door and cut a hole for a hatch at the base, whereby I could slide through Ernest's meals... That's how we coped with his fits. His episodes wielded so much strain on his mind that he feared something terrible could happen, so he'd ask me to lock him up whenever he wasn't feeling right. He admitted in his own words that he could "go too far". He never told me what "go too far" meant, though I suspected the worst. As soon as he felt the warning signs he'd say, I'd better go in the boob. That's what we called the tiny room: the boob. Make sure you bolt the door, he insisted. He would be pacing up and down in the room all night. I got used to it. That's who Ernest was... I loved him, and I still love him, and when you love someone, you care for them, no matter the circumstances.

We found a fleeting sense of stability. Anyone else would have deemed his situation unbearable. There was no room for people like Ernest in a mental hospital. In such a place, they'd keep you for a week or so, give you a few tablets and send you home. Back to your life, your ghosts, your nightmares. When Ernest left St Vincent's Hospital, he was given mood stabilisers. He took his tablets for a while and then stopped taking them, believing he could lead a normal life again through the strength he derived from his art. I believed it for a long time too, up until the day I realised he would never get better.

I had taken it upon myself to help him. He's an exceptional painter and he simply has to paint. Without his art, life would be insufferable. I supported him financially. His family wrote him off. His father forbade him to even visit Longland. I paid for all his expenditures – the canvasses, the brushes and paints, the taxis and hotel rooms. Perhaps my devotion, my persistent concern for him drove him off... one day he decided to move out. He lived alone for a couple of years, and then a woman called Annette moved in with him. At some point, something serious happened between them. I never knew the crux of the story. Did he "go too far"? He must have, as he was committed again, this time for six months.

His mental illness has a strange control over him. After an episode, he doesn't remember a thing... Yes, I saw that when we lived together. As sad as it sounds, once he was back to his usual self, he would knock three times on the door and say, are you going to keep me in the boob for ever, you bastard? I'd unbolt the door, we'd hug. I pretended not to notice his blood-shot eyes and blotchy face. We would laugh. Sometimes he'd look at me with surprise, wondering what had happened.

After his parents' death he shifted back to Longland. Annette was gone and now Brit had entered his life. That was twelve years ago... We hadn't seen much of each other until recently... He would ring me every three months or so to ask whether his work was selling. He would say he was over life in the city, the noise, the traffic, the rabble, as he called it. I didn't think it was such a good move going back to that old house. He hadn't been happy down there, but it seemed to me that he was somehow trying to recover the status he had been robbed of by his father...

I tried to talk to Lucie that Sunday night. I didn't want to unnerve her, but rather to open her eyes to Ernest's struggle. She knew something wasn't right, of course, but he's a hard man to figure out. You've met him, so you know how charming and captivating he can be.

He's inspiring too. His charisma draws artists, eccentrics and bohemians to him, his circle of friends opened up my world. If it were not for

Ernest and his liberated "freaks", I would have been stranded in a mainstream crowd, blending in like everybody else... My cool, scholarly approach to art was turned upside down by Ernest's visceral nature. Even today, he's the only person whose conversation, when it comes to art, still excites me.

Of course, it's not just Ernest's vision that drives him, but also his ego. Ambition consumes him. He's a calculating one when it comes to tracking down helpful contacts, influential journalists. He's even been known to lie to his best friend to serve his interests.

The party was supposedly for Lucie, but in my opinion, it was a means for Ernest to bring back useful acquaintances and resurrect his career.

And, as is often the way with Ernest, he needs too much alcohol, too much Benzedrine, too many uppers, and of course, the women... I know the ugly side of Ernest, a lubricious ogre ready to devour his own children to get what he wants.

The jacket? You would like to have Lucie's jacket? I was hoping to give it back to her in person.

The brooch? No, I don't know how that horrible thing ended up in the grass. Who knows? Maybe it fell off the jacket, maybe Lucie threw it there...

Lucie is complex and secretive. Something had gone wrong with Ernest, I could tell, and I was concerned. I wondered too if it had something to do with Raph. Who knows what he might have told her? Ernest's brother is bitter and twisted, rotten to the core. He hates Ernest and badmouths him at every opportunity... All I can add was that the house was silent and Ernest was sound asleep in his bed, when I left with Rosy, Nicole and June.

Paula Rieter
Cours de l'Intendance
Bordeaux
France

Good afternoon, Paula Rieter speaking. I would like to talk to Officer Lawson, please. It's urgent…

Hello, Officer Lawson, my name is Paula Rieter... Rieter, yes, R-I-E-T-E-R... Inspecteur Agnelli from Poitiers gave me your number... I have crucial information regarding Lucie Bruyère... I received, this morning, a parcel from Inspecteur Agnelli with some of the papers belonging to Lucie… Yes, you remember the papers you found at Mr Renfield's and sent to Inspecteur Agnelli... Amongst the papers, I found a letter addressed to me, a letter Lucie never sent. It was unopened… What Lucie writes is distressing. Let me translate it to you. It speaks for itself.

Longland,
Le premier Mai,
Fête du Travail, Fête du muguet,

Dearest Paula,

It's the first of May. I wonder what the weather is like in Bordeaux. Are there people down your street selling lilies of the valley? My mother grew those delicate flowers in a wide garden-bed. Intoxicating. A procession of white bells hiding in their folds of green leaves. My mother died exactly one year ago. I miss her. I would have liked to be by her side when she died. When she was alive we couldn't stop fighting. She was a dotty old woman. Now, I wish I could hear her voice.

I thought I was strong and that I would overcome any adversity. But I was wrong. Two years ago, Ernest asked me to move in with him, and I said yes. That was a mistake. I turned my back on my friends, my family, my job and my country. My bearings vanished overnight and now, I'm lost. I have never been so miserable. I haven't found the courage to tell you the truth. I don't think I should send you this letter. I love you too much to worry you with what I'm going through. I didn't know what I wanted when I left, for there was so much confusion in my life. I listened to you, to my mother, to my sisters, but all of you were pulling me in different directions and I didn't know what I wanted at the time.

Life with Ernest has not been easy and the signs were there early on. I realised there was a serious problem with him about four months into our relationship. One day in Sydney, as we were going out to a restaurant, a man walked past us and gave us a smile. Ernest got furious, so furious that he confronted the man, screaming absurd accusations at him. When I tried to pacify him, telling him the smile had been innocent, he directed his fury at me. I was scared and embarrassed and I clearly remember thinking: this man has another side to him. It has taken me nearly two years to come back to square one and admit that, yes, there is something wrong with Ernest. But now life has turned into hell. I wake in anguish each morning to a new conflict. Ernest is constantly on my back. The steak is too well done, the potatoes too mushy, the eggs never runny enough for his toast soldiers. A stain on the napkin. A streak on the tablecloth. No milk in the fridge. He blames me for the supermarket mixing up delivery times. The list is endless. Every night he rifles through the kitchen bin, looking for proof of my misdoings. I get scolded in the morning if I have wasted the smallest morsel of food. As hard as I try, Ernest is never happy. I constantly question my own actions. Have I said something wrong? Have I disappointed him? What began as anxiety has now become a constant fear of being caught out. Ernest's anger could break out any time. If I say I miss my country, Ernest will retort in a mocking tone that no one forced me to come to Australia. If I say I miss my family, he will say that I hated my mother and that my sisters are not worth being missed. More and more, I retreat into silence.

He insists that Australia has given me a golden opportunity to make a new start and I haven't risen to the challenge. Australia is a lucky country, how could I pretend it is not? If I should dare cry in front of him, he looks at me with utter contempt. Or he will come up close to me, look into my eyes and say in a detached voice, I worry for you, Lucie Bruyère. Every time he comes in close, yes, every time, I hope he'll show some kindness. But there's never a word of comfort as he walks away. If I should dare slash my wrists in front of him, he would ask me to go and do it outside, so my blood doesn't stain the carpet.

He's always considerate with visitors. That's the paradox: I'm treated awfully when he's all smiles with strangers, especially women. He makes phone calls in the morning, barters with art dealers, chit-chats with his admirers, fixes a date for an interview, greets his models at the door, just after an early lunch, then gets stuck into his work. He doesn't reappear until nightfall. After a quick dinner, he collapses into bed. Meanwhile, I cry my days away.

Am I weak? Am I broken? Am I worthless? Is there something wrong with me? I never imagined I would end up like this. I am neither alive nor dead. There is nothing to comfort me, no one to talk to. No neighbour, no friend. I shuffle about in an alien house in an alien land. The house is huge, you wouldn't believe it, still, I have no room of my own. Ernest is tight to the point of cutting the heating down to just his studio and the kitchen, where I am forced to work. Last summer I tried the caretaker's house, but when the winter came it was damp and cold and I was constantly sniffling.

The trip to France has nearly bled me of all my savings. I use what's left in my bank account to rent my piano. In three months, all my money will be gone. I considered taking a job in the nearby village, but Ernest refuses to let me drive his car and there is a good five kilometres of steep road to get there. The last twelve months have been so hard, I've become a wreck. I've lost weight. I try to avoid the ghost in the mirror. I'm a different person, you wouldn't recognise me. Ernest is killing the best in me.

When Ernest shows a bit of kindness, which seldom happens, I become overwhelmed, hoping the nightmare is about to end. He says he loves me. It lasts two, three days, but then they come again, the off-hand remarks, the dirty looks, the scoffing. I feel I'm living with Dr Jekyll and Mr Hyde.

Ernest's anger goes in cycles. He regularly gets worked up to a state of fury for no apparent reason, then he locks himself in his tower for several days. When he reappears, he has a mad look about him and seems unaware of who I am.

The expression on his face and the sound of his voice are petrifying. Yes, Paula, I'm scared of him. He's like a beast lurking about the house, ready to pounce. Is he sick? Should he be on medication? Does he pretend to be mad? I'm not even sure he's aware of what he's doing. Why has he chosen me? I've come to the conclusion that there is something wrong with me. It must be written all over my face. I must be weak, as Ernest constantly repeats.

Being around him disgusts me. Lying down by his side disgusts me. Sex with him disgusts me. Ernest stinks. His flabby body, the stench of his breath and the rank smell of his skin make me nauseous.

I walk in the forest. I watch the birds. You wouldn't believe how beautiful they are. You remember, I wanted to be a poet. I wanted to be published. I'm tired, Paula, I'm worn out. After two years of this life, I've had enough. I should run away, but somehow I feel paralysed, spellbound. Just putting this letter together has been a huge effort. I try to make sense of my life, but it's a mishmash of fear, sadness, loneliness. Ernest has drained all joy, whatever youth I had left, and energy, from me. When I get told off, I cower like a beaten dog.

Ernest drums into me that I haven't achieved anything, that I'm a disgrace to look at. He might be right. He might be wrong. I don't know. I have no spirit left to disagree. There's no one around here to confide in, no support. I've met Nicole, though, an intelligent French woman. We call each other every week. I haven't told her the truth, but I'm sure she knows something is not right.

My writing isn't going well. All that once gave meaning to my life is lost. I've tried to put together my notes on Jean Lucien but I'm unable to concentrate. I stare at the pages, read them but can't decipher their meaning. Would you believe it? I can't understand a word of it. Music is my only friend. When I feel I'm going mad, I play. Thanks to Schubert, I haven't lost my mind yet. I wonder where my dreams have gone.

If I knew how to pray I would, but I don't know whom to ask for help.

Your friend always,
Lucie

The letter stops here... Sorry, I didn't want to cry but I cannot help it... Lucie never told me what was going on, but I always knew she was not telling the truth. I should have listened to my gut feeling.

Brock Olsen
Police Station
Watooga
New South Wales

You've got to let me go, man... I haven't done anythin' wrong. Jesus, I earned that cash fair and square. I work three days a week at Heavens Bar... Yep, in Thirroul. Call 'em! They'll tell you...

No way, you've got to be kidding! Am I dreamin' or what? Me mum found it under the bed? She reckons I stole it. She came here yesterday to hand it in. What the... Me own mum? She ratted me to the cops. Man, that's low. You've got to be a sicko to do that.

Yeah, that's right, I got a waiter's gig at Renfield's. He needed two of us. How did I know 'bout the party? Me girlfriend heard on the grapevine. Yeah, Lydia's me girlfriend... Nah, she isn't my sister. We said we were brother and sister to get the gig. Lydia thought we should take the job and get some cash to piss off to Byron Bay. Just the two of us. I was fine with that.

Lydia called Renfield and asked him if he needed two youngsters to wait on his guests. She was real cool on the phone. 'Cos when you say "young", you're pretty sure Renfield's gonna to take the bait. Everyone knows he likes 'em young. Yeah, Renfield, he's a dirty pig. So we went to his place. Lydia looked super hot. She'd put on a stack of make-up and she wore a mini-skirt. Renfield had a good look at her and said, I'm really impressed by young people who want to work on weekends... He even asked Lydia if she wanted to model for his paintings. She said she'd never done it, but she'd love to have a crack. He was drooling over her tits. Sure enough we got the job. Easy peasy.

On the day, I parked me banger near the house. Renfield came out of nowhere and yelled that we had to move. This was the carpark for guests. Fuckin' snob!

What was the party like? Oh man, lots of wackos and weirdos. Heaps of drugs, rich people's gear. They were doin' lines in the bathroom. Renfield got really plastered. He's a nutcase... I saw him in one of the rooms with an old boiler... Nah, not the Frog. A flabby troll with a stupid paper hat stuck on her head... They were havin' a good time. No bull.

What was I doing there? Snooping around? Come on, get off me back. I just opened the door and there he was, leaning against the table, and she was on her knees. I saw the orange paper hat going up and down. I nearly burst out laughin'.

What did she have on? A red dress, I think... Nah, I wouldn't know her name... Oh, yeah, maybe, hang on a sec, one time she came to the kitchen for a glass of water. She said she had some art gallery in Sydney. Yeah, I remember now...

Nah, don't know if anyone else saw Renfield and her together... What else? Geez, you ask a lot of questions. I saw that guy too, Gary, he came through the back door when Lydia and I were half-asleep, our heads on the kitchen table, waiting for the party to end. He scared the shit out of us. His clothes were wet. He said he'd had too much to drink and fallen in the lake. I laughed. What an idiot! Yeah, we had a chat. He hung around for ages...

What? I told you man, I'm no thief! You really don't let go, do ya? I haven't done nothin'... Me father? What about him? You wanna call him? Not me father, mate, he's insane! He'll fully kill me! He'll bash me, beat me to death! Please, don't call him. I'll tell you what really went on... It was Lydia. None of this shit would have happened if it wasn't for that moll. It was her idea.

That party was full on. The whole time we were there, we were busy, with the Frog ordering us around. I reckon she thought we were a couple of retards. Mate, she was pissed off about something.

Maybe she'd seen the old slag blowing her fella... But Lydia and I didn't muck about. We did the foods, ran to the big room with more booze, dashed back to the kitchen, washed dirty glasses.

The Frog? What was she doing? Putting stuff in the microwave, going outside for a smoke... We were doin' another round with the booze when Lydia spotted him, that creepy Renfield brother. Lydia saw that dopehead sneak out of the library, all red and sweaty, with a suss look on his face. See mate, that's the room where all the guests had left their bags and coats and stuff... Could have been three-thirty, everyone was off their heads, dancin' up and down the stairs... The Renfield brother didn't come back to the party and Lydia was sure he'd taken off with the loot. That's when she said we should check out the library too. Could be more stuff to nick, she said. I told her I didn't wanna to do it, but Lydia said, look at them, they're shitfaced, who's gonna notice? I told her to get lost. She wouldn't let it go. Before I knew it, she stuck her tongue down me throat. Next thing she had me on the look-out while she fished around in the library. She came out happy as Larry, with seven hundred bucks stuffed down her bra.

Huh? How long? Took her fifteen minutes, maybe. The dopehead had cleaned out the hand bags, but there was a sports bag under the couch. The moron didn't see it, she yelled. Yippee! We're rich! She gave me the cash. I ran to the car and hid it in the glovebox, then rushed back to the kitchen. We kept servin' the booze. Sweet as. That's it. Nothing more to say...

What time did we leave? Well we pissed off with everyone else. When Lydia saw they were all goin' she said we'd better join the pack. What time was that? Would have been four-thirty...

What now? What's gonna to happen to me? Charged with theft? You go to court for that? Hang on a sec, I told you, it's fucking Lydia. She wanted to go to Byron Bay...

Nah, we didn't pinch nothin' else. I swear. Credit cards? You crazy? No way, that's criminal! I've never touched a credit card in me life.

We nicked seven hundred bucks, that's right, got busted, that's right, but we didn't steal credit cards. I knew we'd get in trouble... And me mother, she isn't any better. Dobbed me in. That's low.

Act V

Ernest Renfield
Longland
New South Wales

I've been waiting for you... I've been waiting, and here you are... Finally! Come in, quick, come inside! I'm so glad to see you. Let me look at you, my friend. Might I call you my friend at present? Are you my friend? Could we call ourselves good friends? Yes? Yes, you said and I'm pleased... Do come in. By the way, I'm sorry if I got a bit worked up last time we saw each other. Really sorry... I've been angry too many times lately... When I saw you had issued a search warrant, I cut loose and I'm sure you can understand why...

Do you know that you bear a very beautiful name? Lawson, the Son of the Law, a name so suited to who you are. I haven't been so lucky. My parents called me Ernest! Me? Can you believe it? As if I ever wanted to be earnest!

Why don't we sit in my studio for a change? I've lit the wood-stove and heaved a good supply of logs upstairs. We won't be cold! Let's go the short way; via the backstairs... First to the kitchen, you know how to get there, that's right, to the left... You're almost at home here now... And down the corridor... Yes, this way... See, behind that door are the old backstairs. This is my shortcut. Don't tell anyone... Watch out, it's narrow and steep... Oh, my knees! Too much weight, I should go on a diet. I'm too lazy for that. Too lazy to cook greens, veggies, you know what I mean. I live off frozen stuff... Then go left, now down the passage. Yes, to the very end... Another flight of stairs... Ouch! Nearly there. Careful with the last couple of steps... They are treacherous... Here we are... Please, take a seat... I'm sure you'll have a drop of something. Yes? Did I hear a yes? Goodo! I knew you'd surrender to it *in fine*. What would you fancy? I have an excellent cognac. Want a drop? You won't be disappointed... No, no, sit here, in the armchair, you'll get a better view...

My head is better, thank you. A superficial cut. No broken bones luckily. Like the forest? It's amazing isn't it? See how dense. A jungle, impenetrable, dark, cold, musty, damp, like a cathedral with a vaulted ceiling and high architraves. Did you know that Longland Road, which runs across the valley, is the only way to get in and out of here? Good cognac, isn't it? Feeling giddy already? You'll remember this day!

Well, well, well... More questions... Did I hear two gunshots around five o'clock in the morning after the party? Two gunshots? Let me think... Let me think... Yes, I did actually... And today I'll be honest with you, Officer Lawson, I didn't go straight to bed after my last guests had left, as I stated a few weeks ago... The truth would have been somehow too embarrassing to divulge... But it would be stupid to feel ashamed in the company of a good friend, wouldn't it? Do you know what the real proof of friendship is? Well, a true friend is someone to whom you can tell the truth. So, today I'm going to tell you honestly what happened on that Sunday night... Rather, that Monday morning...

It was close enough to five. The sky had started to whiten. I was about to go to bed when Lucie showed up at the door. She looked... goodness me, how to describe her... she looked as though she'd been fighting for her life. Her hair was wet. Her dress, torn on one side, was covered in mud. Her face of a bluish white and her lips dark from the cold... What else? Oh yes, she was barefoot. In a word, she looked as though she'd been attacked by a gang of criminals. What are you doing downstairs, she hissed. You aren't in bed yet? She certainly didn't look very happy to see me, or maybe, she had something else in mind and I was in her way.

What happened to you, I asked. Have you been for a swim, have you been assaulted in the park?

She opened her eyes wide and glared at me. I didn't say anything at that point, just stared daggers back at her and waited for the next episode of her little drama to unfold. She loves to put on a show. That's Lucie. She waits for her white knight to come to her rescue. But eh, I've been caught too many times. I thought to myself, enough is enough. Let's wait and see. I'm not going to budge. Of course, what I expected to happen did happen… Ernest, I'm going to leave you, she said. I shrugged. That wasn't a surprise. I knew she was up to something. Too many furtive talks with Nicole… Telephone calls suddenly interrupted when I stepped too close… Lots of plotting and planning… But honestly, I thought it was the best outcome for both of us. I even felt relieved. Thereupon she marched towards the library. She walked in, closed the door and reappeared five minutes later in dry clothes, wearing a pair of jeans, a jumper and a green parka. She threw her dress at my face, and said again, Ernest I'm leaving you. I answered, well, good bye, Little Miss. If you want to go, then off you go, farewell! Nobody is going to stop you… She looked baffled. You are going to let me go? You don't want to talk? Talk! Talk! She always wants to talk! I've lost track of how many times she dredged up that spiel. Talk about what? I asked. There's nothing to talk about.

There she was, standing like an imbecile in the middle of the room, looking at me. Open your bag, I asked, and show me what's in it! She didn't get it, and I had to explain, Lucie dear, this wouldn't be the first time I've been stitched up by a Little Miss like you... I need to be sure that you haven't stolen any valuables, that's all... She started crying. I grabbed hold of her travelling bag to check what was crammed inside. Jumpers, jeans, runners, toiletries. As I zipped open a side pocket she wailed, where is my money? I had seven hundred dollars in there! You've stolen my money! I swore that I hadn't taken a cent and asked her to quieten down. People were asleep upstairs. You've got to be naive to leave such a large amount of money in a bag that doesn't lock, I explained. She kept crying. As I searched the travelling bag a second time I hit upon a book, one of mine, of course... Just as you would expect from this sort of woman. See this, I said, brandishing the book, this isn't yours! The book stays here, if you don't mind. It was *The Prophet* by Kahlil Gibran. I purchased it in London a long time ago. First edition, printed in 1923. I have always been a bibliophile and a fine collector. You've seen my library downstairs, haven't you? Keep your book, Lucie sneered. Then she took off the emerald ring that I'd given her, quite an expensive one, and threw it at me. Your ugly ring… blah, blah, blah… something in French… God knows what she was saying…

For a moment or so, she seemed embarrassed, though soon enough she began to plead again. Why did I ask her to come to Australia to share my life? Why did I lie to her? Yes, she called me a liar. Have you noticed that people who call you a liar are those best at lying? She had been conspiring for weeks to run away, ready to take off like a thief, plotting to leave me without being gutsy enough to let me know the truth, and now, I was the one who was called a liar. Who is the liar, I pressed. She wasn't listening to me. She was eyeballing my every move. She looked frightened, yes, frightened, as if I was about to grab her and slap her around. By George! I've never hit a woman in my life. Men who raise a hand on a woman are lowlifes, if you want my opinion. They should be given a taste of their own medicine… Eventually she managed to stop her weeping and launched into a long address. Oh yes, she's good at making endless speeches… I'll cut it short for you, or it'll take me all day.

I was expecting you'd ask me to stay here, she whined. I was thinking you'd kiss me and apologise for your harsh words, your indifference, your selfishness. I was expecting to hear that you love me, that you never lied to me, that we were going to build a happy future together. Supporting each other. Understanding each other. I'll spare you the remainder of the homily, Officer Lawson. What a nerve! Blaming me for my harsh words, when they haven't had any other purpose than to toughen her up. She's always lived in cotton wool... My so-called indifference comes from the fact that by remaining outwardly distant, I have bypassed many conflicts with her. As for my selfishness, or what women call selfishness, it's more a question of survival... If I want to keep painting I must be selfish. I have no sentimentality, that's right. I hate getting maudlin. And yes, everything is thrown down the grinder for my work, yes, I must use all the means at my disposal, even if it includes her, her life, her energy... But what she doesn't get, what none of these brainless birds get, is that I'm also thrown down the same grinder, spending up my time, my energy, my health, my life.

Yet I explained calmly, you haven't understood me, Lucie dear. A happy married life doesn't suit me. Plucking away at daisies to work out if you love me or love me not isn't my ideal. We don't have to hold each other's hand to have a fulfilling life. You wait for me to make you happy. Why don't you find happiness through your own means? Why do you have to rely on me all the time? If I'm fine, you are fine. If I'm angry, you tremble and cry. Why is that? I thought women had become liberated by now! Is that what married life is supposed to be, making a good job at stifling one another? Look, you've stolen a wisdom book. Rather let's just say you took the book in order to read it and forgot to put it back in my library... Have you started reading it? Then I told her that if she hadn't yet read it, she'd better listen up.

Lawson, can you grab the book? It's there, over there, on that little table. Would you mind passing it over to me? I wanted to take a look at it yesterday. Such a good read... Yes, I chose to read the few lines that are self-explanatory: "Love one another but make not a bond of love. Give your hearts, but not into each other's keeping. For only the hand of life can contain your hearts. And stand together yet not too near together. For the pillars of the temple stand apart. And the oak tree and the cypress grow not in each other's shadow." Isn't that beautifully put?

As she stood in the middle of the room, I asked, do you understand what it means? She shook her head and started crying again. Obviously, she hadn't been listening to me. She looked so miserable, so stupid, like a pig-headed child you'd like to give a good shake. I found her self-abasement infuriating. She stood there, her arms to the side, her bag at her feet. She kept looking around, in a daze, as though she couldn't make up her mind.

You want to go, then clear off, I finally said. You should learn to be more assertive. You shouldn't put so much faith in people. Let me give you an example... You trusted the two young people who came here to wait on our guests, but just have a look around! Notice anything? She gazed about as if seeing the room for the first time. It looked as if a bomb had gone off. Yes, what a mess, you are right, she agreed without conviction. Were the waiters not paid to clean up too, she whimpered? I've told you on other occasions, you pay people when the work is done, not before, I replied. You made a point of paying these two loafers when they arrived. Two kids, could they have really been so difficult to handle? Why didn't you keep an eye on them? Take a look at the white couch. You know how much it cost? If you'd been around you would have done something, wiped away the wine when it was still wet, instead, you were outside smoking, but now, God knows how they'll be able to remove that terrible stain...

She kept her head down and mumbled, I'm sorry. Yes, sorry, she was sorry. That's all she could think of, all she could say. I was tired of looking at her… And that's more or less where our story ends, Officer Lawson.

Except for one last thing, shortly after our argument, as I was sliding the book back on the library shelf, voices broke out on the terrace. I recognised Gary's. He was leading the party. Nicole and Rosy were on his heels. Lucie caught a glimpse of them. She became panicky, quickly packing her stuff. I followed her in order to avoid any embarrassing questions. We ran down the passage, entered the sitting-room and she left through the back door. Yes, she left. She left me. End of a beautiful love story… She vanished as a young doe whose colours fade away. The catbirds were wailing like newborn babies. The kookaburras were laughing at the first rays of the sun. I dashed back to my bedroom via the backstairs, the stairs we've taken today to come here… I ripped off my jacket and my shirt, and quickly put on my pyjamas. The party was already half-way up the main staircase. No time to take off my pants. So I jumped into bed and lay there. They walked into my bedroom. Gary checked me out. I didn't budge. Oh yes… I forgot… The two gunshots? Well, as I was lying in my bed, at that very moment, I heard, Bang! Bang! It was coming from the forest… Game poachers. They hunt deer at that time of the year. Some people like deer meat. Well, I don't... I find it too heavy. It gives me a stomach ache.

Well, that's all I have to say, Officer Lawson... There is nothing more to add to the story, I'm afraid...

Now, you understand why I didn't divulge a word of Lucie's caper when we met the first time... The truth would have been too humiliating. Backing up Nicole's testimony by reporting Lucie as a missing person was the lesser of two evils; better for me and better for Lucie. I believe she has suffered enough setbacks in France already with her previous partners, with her family, in her job, yes, it was less hurtful for her and for everyone else...

Raphaël Renfield
Australian Federal Police
Brisbane Headquarters
Queensland

Gimme a break! You'll find what you're looking for in Longland... In the old caretaker's house... I took none of those fucking credit cards! I couldn't. Even if I'm broke, I'm not a crook. I haven't got a pot to piss in. Sunnybank Motorbikes? That's a lot of bull. I sold it ages ago, live off the dregs. So get off my case, will you? Ever been broke? Any idea what it's like? It sucks!

I went to Ernest's because I've got no one else to ask... I called him on the Wednesday before the party. I said I'd come early to have a chat, biting my tongue, telling him I just wanted to catch up. I didn't want to rub him up the wrong way. With Ernest, you've got to know how to work him. I borrowed a mate's suit and tie and pulled into Longland around five. Parked the rattle-trap out of sight, on the side of the road, a few hundred metres from the entrance. I didn't want to look like a complete bum. Ernest walked me to the sitting-room. He poured us both a drink. He sat there, spivved up in his black suit, like Lord Muck. I looked around. My mother used to sit where Ernest was sitting, with her feet to the fire. In the same armchair. The fireplace still had a whiff of burnt wood and soot...

After a while I stopped daydreaming and said, look, Ernest, I've been down and out lately. I haven't paid my board in two months. Could you lend me two grand? I'll pay you back in a couple of months... He kept sipping on his drink, waited, kept me hanging for a little longer eventually spitting, I can't help you, Raph.

Blood is thicker than water, they say. Well, that's crap. When it comes to me and Ernest, anything is thicker than blood! Every man for himself, more like... Thanks for nothing, I blurted, now, I'm good to sleep on the street. He added in his conniving way, so much like him, I wouldn't mind helping you, Raph, but I'm in dire financial straits myself... As if! He's a tight cunt. He has money, of course he does. How much for a party like this, eh? I saw the booze and the grub stacked up in the kitchen. How much do you shell out for that sort of a spread? Honestly, two grand, it's no big deal to him. I was fuming...

Anyways, we just sat there, facing each other. Ernest had his back to the corridor. I kept looking around... The fireplace, the metal cabinet, my old man's desk. I was about to have another crack. I needed the money so badly. Then I saw the prick looking at my shoes. Yeah, my shoes! The suit and the tie looked sort of okay, but my shoes... they were my old shoes. I haven't bought a pair of shoes in donkey's years, haven't needed to. Then I looked down at my feet and realised I wasn't wearing socks... Fuck! No socks... I tried to slide my feet back under the chair. For Christ's sake, I thought, while the old bastard kept staring at my feet, smirking. Yeah, he smirked... Oh man... I got so pissed off. And then I thought to myself, Raph, you're not going back to Brissie without your moolah. You're not going to waste a twelve-hour drive and four-hundred bucks in petrol... no way. In two hours' time the place will be packed with rich pigs. All cashed-up. Megabucks. What about doing the dirty deed? Yeah, the credit cards, the loot...

You've got to understand, Officer... When you're down to your last buck, you'll do anything. Anything! Anyway, I was about to finish my drink. I looked up and saw her... Yep, Lucie. She was sneaking down the corridor with a small bag. Quiet as a mouse. When she heard us in the sitting-room she turned right around and darted back. Ernest didn't notice a thing. Then I twigged... That chick was about to fly the coop. I looked at Ernest and stifled a laugh: you throw a big do and the bride-to-be is about to fuck off. Hah, hah.

But I played it down. Watched Ernest finish his drink, left the room and went outside for a ciggie. The first guests showed up. Fur-coats, leather jackets, Louis Vuitton bags. Wowee! I was over the moon... I had a couple of beers, not too much, didn't want to get blotto. I sweated it out. And around three o'clock, when they were all off their heads conga-dancing up and down the stairs, I made my way to the library. That's where they'd tossed their bags and rags. Cool as a cucumber I ruffled through and pocketed as much as I could... Cash, credit cards, driver's licences, everything, yeah, driver's licences, they're good too.

Huh? What time was that? Around three... I notched my belt tight, stuffed the loot down the front of my shirt, and jumped out the window. I jumped out that window heaps of times as a kid. Then I ran up towards the forest... No, I didn't take the main path to the car. A fire trail goes uphill and leads to the road. I know these woods like the back of my hand.

As I came near the old caretaker's house, I heard a cry inside. Then another cry, from further away. I thought I'd better fuck off before some dude ratted on me to the cops, but I couldn't move. It was bloody weird, my legs were kind of heavy, like I'd grown roots. I knew I shouldn't have come back to bloody Longland. I broke into a sweat...

I thought of my mum and dad and Sunday church... I hated myself for coming here and was shitting myself about getting sprung. My legs were like jelly, but I forced myself to move and ran to the caretaker's house. I got inside, stripped off my shirt and unloaded what I'd nicked into the gap in the old bricked-in fireplace. I knew about the loose bricks, 'cos that's where I used to stash ciggies and pornos when I was a kid... Yeah, I threw what I'd swiped in there... You can go and check. I'm no thief. You'll find all the gear inside. I know, I'm no choir boy. I've done some stupid stuff. I like doing deals. I like my gambling too, but I'm not an idiot, and I'm not that bad either...

Ernest's rotten. I remember the day my old man went to town on him. Best thing my dad ever did. Good on him... Why? Because of his filthy ways. I haven't got much morals, I'm a hood, but Ernest! Parties, alcohol, hard drugs, women and men. Yep, men! He likes men too. He's a homo. Even when he was a kid... I saw him at it. Took my mum's nightie and made airs and graces in front of the mirror. Looked like a clown. How do you call them people? Travesties? Transvestites? Is that right? Gives me the creeps. See, that Gary, that fag, they've been together, I'm sure he's been with that Polack… And at the party, when he was outside having a smoke I stayed well away. Backs to the wall, as they say…

That's what my parents couldn't stand, Officer. My old man did what he could to steer him back to a normal life. See, my father was tough but righteous. But even as a kid, Ernest was a little lecher… He tried that shit on our neighbour's son. The lad was just a couple of years younger. But it wasn't to the kid's taste and he dobbed him in. My old man went berserk. He and my uncle waited all day for Ernest to come home. He turned up at nightfall and my father grabbed him by the hair, started whacking him about the head. Real hard. He gave him the full treatment. But you know what? The sleazy bastard didn't scream. Didn't make a sound… If my uncle hadn't stopped him, my father would have killed Ernest. Dad gave him a good bashing, he did.

But you've got to understand, Officer, Ernest was vicious. He was cruel to dogs, cats, birds, chooks, anything that came across his path… One day in the hen-house he throttled eight tiny little chicks. For no reason. Let me tell you, my father should have wiped him out… Yeah, my father tried to put him on the straight and narrow… And you know what? When he was fifteen, my father was about to go for him, can't remember what Ernest had done this time, but the scumbag raised his fist: you lay another finger on me and I'll smash you to pieces! Yep, that's what he said.

My parents tried to give us a good upbringing. They took us to mass each week. But from the start, Ernest was a waste of space. Piece of shit... My mother spent the last years of her life crying. She said that if she'd known such a "profligate" would see the light of day, she'd have killed herself...

Yeah, as I said, I was pretty sure Lucie was about to piss off. Like all them girls he's scared away. He's got a long list of sheilas in his trophy cabinet. Those who nicked off before it was too late were the smart ones. Annette, she had a brain. You've never heard of Annette? Ah, she's the one who came before Lucie... Hang on! No... Brit came before Lucie, Annette before Brit... Difficult to keep track... How do I know? I just happen to know... Annette ran off... That was a wise move. Yep, I was glad when I saw the Frog was about to clear off... She's not a bad girl...

Do I know Annette? Yeah, I met her... As I said, a smart woman. She worked for the Sydney Festival. Real smart. She fled the nest when she was five months pregnant... Yeah, pregnant by Ernest... He never told you? Sure, Ernest has a son. He's about ten years old. Lives with his mum. Ernest has been denied access. No contact. Not even a supervised visit, considering his past... Never told you he had a son? Never told you he "had a past" either? Well, that's no surprise! He'll do anything to avoid paying child support...

This Lucie, he made her come all the way from France with a lot of phoney promises... He's cunning as a shit-house rat, he takes advantage of people, he's a swindler... See, these girls, he bamboozles them... I reckon he told Lucie he knew a big-wig in the Immigration Department who'd help her get permanent residency. She got sucked in.

You'd like to know more about Brit and Annette? Ernest didn't talk much about them to me... I actually think he didn't speak much to anyone about them... I wouldn't want to stir up all that shit but since you're asking me... Brit, I knew her. Nice sheila, gorgeous looking. Italian. She was an artist. Real talented. Wanted to make a career for herself. She was into drugs... for inspiration, she said. I gave her a bit of weed once. Ernest gave her the sales pitch, saying he'd be able to set her up for an exhibition in Sydney. She got all excited, moved in with him, did all his cooking and cleaning. She slogged for months on her painting and, at the end of the day, zip! No exhibition. Ernest kept stringing her along. The poor thing gave me a buzz one day.

She was on the skids, yeah, she was losing it. I said, you've got to leave him. Get the fuck out of there. She didn't listen. Then she started to go downhill… sitting all day at the window staring into space. One morning, she ran through the forest to the top of the cliff and jumped. Her body was found two days later, washed away by the waves…

You bet your arse it's terrible… As for Annette, that's another horrible story… Ernest was denied access to the child because he hit her when she was five months pregnant. They lived in a studio in Kings Cross… On the ground floor… She jumped out of the bathroom window and ran away just wearing a tee-shirt and knickers… One of your boys in blue found the poor bird the following morning, half-frozen in a back lane… No, she didn't lodge a restraining order against him… Too scared… Ernest is sick, believe me… So yes, he's got a son and I hope he doesn't take after his father… We aren't honourable sons, one a stray dog and the other a thief. My parents are better off dead, I tell you…

Get real! I wouldn't dream of getting Lucie in trouble with Ernest. She came up to me when I was outside. We had a bit of a chat. She asked me to keep my mouth shut… She knew I'd seen her in the corridor with her travelling bag. I gave her my word, of course. I'm down to my last buck, I said. She set off, came back and slipped a hundred in my pocket. I gave her my phone number. She promised to visit me in Queensland. She's not a bad bird for a Frog.

Rosy Barth
Australian Federal Police
Sydney Headquarters
New South Wales

Yes, you're quite correct, I did lose my wallet. Sorry, I forgot... I'm confused, but my wallet wasn't in my handbag when I looked for the torch...Yes, thank you, I wouldn't mind a tissue...

Why did I go to the party, given I don't like Ernest? Yes, I loathe him... I can't believe I allowed it to happen. I wish I'd never been to that bloody party... Yes, that's the truth... we had sex... that's true. In the sitting-room... I'm so ashamed of myself. Lucie might've seen us. It might've sent her crazy. The whole thing could have been my fault. Well, let's face it... I panicked. I didn't want to be found out... I couldn't bear what I'd done, being fucked around again by that man, no, I couldn't bear it... Last time I talked to you... well... I lied... I played stupid... I thought you'd believe me.

Sorry, yes, my wallet... That's right. We were outside... It was so cold... I told Gary and Nicole I'd go back. I went up the path to the house, then up the stairs. The glass doors were wide open. The party room was a complete mess. I zigzagged my way through, and as I was about to enter the library, I heard two voices arguing. They belonged to Ernest and Lucie.

I walked discreetly along the corridor. The sitting-room door was ajar... There were no guests around. Ernest had his back to me. Lucie was leaning against the wall. She was holding on to a large bag. I could hardly recognise her. Nothing like the woman I'd met earlier that evening. She looked washed out, completely spent. She was wearing a pair of jeans and a green parka. Her hair was tied back in a ponytail. It looked dirty. After a while, she asked Ernest in a faded voice why he had never told her he had a son... A son? A big surprise for me too! Ernest hissed, how do you know about my son? She said Raphaël had told her. No one talked for a while then Ernest asked if it was all she'd been told. No, she said, Raphaël also told me about your story with Brit. I'm leaving you, she added. There's no hope, no future with you, you'll never change. Ernest laughed and poured himself a large whisky. Then I heard the same ear-bashing that he used to give me whenever we had a serious argument.

Gosh, I had long forgotten about that, but he still had it down pat... You women, you're all the same... Isn't that ironic? You come here, you make yourselves comfortable, you prance at my arm. It makes you feel special, important. It gives meaning to your meaningless life. You prey on my generosity, my kindness, my time. You say you don't want me to change a bit, you say you love me as I am, but that's not true, is it? In the end, if I don't live up to your demands, it's bye-bye... Our Father, who art in Heaven, have you created all women out of the same mould?

Brit, you want to know about Brit, don't you? So, let's talk about poor little Brit. She was a junkie when I met her, flat broke, ill-educated, a wreck covered in sores and pimples. I gave her a chance, helped her get it together. And the very day she got clean, she pissed off!

Lucie was still leaning against the wall, looking as if she was about to collapse. She gave a sigh and said in a sad voice, where did she go? Ernest shook his head... Who cares? She left. That's all that matters. I give you all a chance, and, as soon as I've taught you good manners, how to speak English correctly, how to dress, how to take care of yourself, you get up and leave... And you nick something on your way out... Rosy, Joanna, Annette, Brit, all of you... Looking like cheap sluts. After I've taken care of you, fed you, dressed you, taught you all about art and life, you fuck off. That's how you repay me for my kindness...

When I heard my name on that list, when I

realised I was nothing more than a cheap slut to him, as he put it, I thought, what a miserable low-life you are, Ernest Renfield… And I got so bloody angry, I nearly burst out screaming.

Then I heard Lucie ask if she could leave. Her legs were trembling. Hang on a minute, Ernest growled. I haven't finished with you, Lucie Bruyère…

What? No, of course, Ernest didn't let her go. I know, I was there… He's lying through his teeth. He ordered her to sit down in the armchair and began to tell her off. You've stolen a book from my library… *The Prophet*. See, he said, this is literature. I wonder how a woman as stupid as you is capable of understanding a book like this! Now listen, I'll read you some words of wisdom… Then he opened the book and started reading, his drink in his left hand, the book in his right. Page after page, he kept on reading. I can't remember how long he went on for, but it was gut-wrenching… Lucie was swaying in the armchair, looking as if she was about to pass out. Her eyes were closed. Her face tense, grey, withered. Tears were running down her cheeks, her nose was running.

Ernest finally put the book down and said, okay, you want to know, so I'll tell you. I have a son… His name is Hayden. I've never lost track of him. His mother moved many times, sometimes she shifted overnight. She went to another state, but a couple of reliable friends of mine tailed her. They understand my situation and that Hayden and I cannot lose sight of each other. I need to know where he lives so I can send him a birthday card. And I always sign off with "Your daddy who loves you".

Then Ernest went on explaining how the mother, whom he called a spiteful whore, had persecuted him for many years. He said she was unstable, yes, unstable, and she didn't have what it took to raise a child… Yes, he had warned the Family Court, but that bunch of wigged puppets had always dismissed his plight… His tale would have broken your heart. To me, it sounded like utter bullshit…

Lucie was hunched, her bag squashed on her lap. Her knuckles were white from clenching. Ernest went up to her and grabbed her ponytail, pulling her head back. Don't you think I am a good father, Lucie Bruyère, he said. His voice was harsh, blunt, chilling. Lucie opened her eyes wide. I had to stifle a scream. Seeing Ernest like this was horrifying… I really thought he was going to hurt the poor woman. I couldn't move. Now of course, looking back, I wonder whether I could have done something to stop it, go outside, call for help, but honestly, I was too petrified to move.

Why don't you talk, Ernest asked. You've got

such a talent at lecturing others, and now… nothing. Cat got your tongue?

He put his glass on the table, bent low and took hold of Lucie's jaw in his right hand, forcing her mouth to open.

Yuck, you stink of cigarettes! Why don't you talk now? Say something? Blah, blah, blah… His hand was huge, with bulging veins, massive fingers, and Lucie's face looked brittle in its grip… She scowled as she tried to break free.

You never say a bad word, eh? You never get angry or tell me to piss off. You just stare at me, completely passive. You think you can just walk out the door. Goodbye, nice to have met you… We've spent two years together. I just threw a big party for your ladyship that cost me a fortune. That might be what young people do these days… casual sex… a good fuck… and bye-bye. Well, I'm a bit too old for that shit… sorry. I don't like being made a fool of and, right now, I feel like a damn fool.

Ernest still had Lucie's jaw in a tight hold. She was moaning. I was rigid, short of breath, confronted by a vision from hell. As I looked at that man, I thought, how could this be the man I'd loved, the man I'd been so happy with? He was someone else. The man I'd loved would never assault a woman.

For a moment, I thought Ernest was about to

break her jaw. Lucie let out a scream. I had to bite my hand to stop myself from screaming too.

What a tight, prudish little girl you are, he said… All screwed up because I asked you to join in with me and Rosy? Don't you like Rosy? She's no spring chicken but she's still a bit of alright, don't you think? It got you so worked up that you ran outside and jumped in the lake! Did you want to drown, or put on a little show so someone could rescue you? Poor Little Miss… Poor darling… Aren't you all sexually liberated in France? Wouldn't you like to fondle a juicy slapper like Rosy? No, you wouldn't! I tell you what… I thought you were a sex goddess, but you're nothing like it. You are a fraud, a con artist, a phoney! Fucking you is like fucking dead meat.

I had to pull away then and lean against the wall. Is that what he thought of me? I'd gone from being a golden doe to a juicy slapper! I felt a surge of anger. I thought, you son of a bitch… You're going to pay for that… I clenched my fist… But he is so huge, so strong, and at that moment in a murderous state of mind, yes absolutely, a murderous state of mind… What could I do?

Now Ernest was heaping more insults onto Lucie, calling her frigid, a low-life, an ugly scarecrow… You wouldn't believe how he carried on… For your education, Little Miss, Picasso said there are two kinds of women: goddesses and doormats. And you know why? Because Picasso had read the great Marquis de Sade. Remember Sade? Reading him made you so horny once upon a time... According to Sade, Nature has created strong beings, like me, and weak creatures, like you. Do I have to explain to you what a doormat is? You know that word? That's where you wipe the dirt from your shoes...

Ernest laughed. Lucie was still clinging to her bag. He stepped sideways to try to pick up his glass from the table. In the process, he let go of Lucie. At that very moment she leapt from the armchair, and holding on to her bag, ran to the back door, into the night.

Ernest turned around. Staggering, roaring, as if he were in dreadful pain. He reached for the metal cabinet, opened it, grabbed a rifle. Then he stepped to the threshold of the door, took aim and fired two shots... My heart was thumping... I was terrified that if he happened to see me he'd shoot me dead...

He seemed to realise the two blasts might have woken up his guests... He quickly left the room out the back door. My whole body was shaking. I had drawn blood from my hand by biting it. I stumbled across the room and went outside. Ernest had vanished. I leant against a tree and vomited... The day had dawned. I looked about for any sign of Lucie. She could have been injured or fallen down dead... But she was gone... I hoped with all my heart that she was gone and would stay miles away from that monster... For the rest of her life.

On my way back to the house I saw the rifle, half-concealed in a shrub. I decided to get rid of it... Who knows what Ernest might have done next? He could have gone crazy and wiped out everyone in the house, including me... I grabbed the bloody thing. I couldn't look at it. I could barely hold it. My arm was trembling. I wandered down to the edge of the gully, chucked the rifle in there and ran away.

All that I'd heard and seen that night made me sick. I never thought Ernest could behave like that. Artists and students had spun rumours about Ernest... One of the girls who sat for him many years ago told me once he was more than just mad. I didn't believe her... But the fact was that his models usually sat two or three times and never came back.

I threw the rifle away because I was afraid... Maybe that was a stupid thing to do. As I walked across the sitting-room, I heard Gary and Nicole. They were looking for Ernest. Nicole was carrying her daughter in her arms. The child was sound asleep. I stood in the corridor. I kept what I had just seen to myself. I didn't mention the rifle. Nicole noticed the blood on my hand and around my face. I said I'd cut my hand with a piece of broken glass, quickly wiping my face clean and suggesting we go and check if Ernest was in his bedroom. I was pretty sure he would be there...

Gary Whitehall
Longland
New South Wales

You'd like to know what I'm doing here, wandering at nightfall like a lost soul? Well, Ernest called me early this morning... He asked me to get in the car and come to Longland at once... Goodness me, I never thought I'd have such a hell of a day.

When he rang... it could have been around six o'clock... I was still asleep. I wondered what on earth had happened. I thought maybe Lucie had come home. But Ernest didn't want to talk on the phone. I got dressed and drove off. When I arrived, he was having his breakfast. He was surprisingly calm. He walked me to the kitchen without a word. Everything about Longland seemed back to normal, though I did notice Lucie's piano was gone. I didn't ask why. We sat in the kitchen and had a coffee. Gary, he said to me, I'm going on an important trip and I might be gone a while. You're my best friend and the only person I can trust. Here are my keys... This one is for the front door; that one for the back; the little one, for my studio. You might not know it, but the door to the studio was broken recently. I had it repaired...

Well, I didn't ask why, but I'd heard about the search warrant and noticed the cut above his right eye. So, I pieced things together regarding the broken door... I guess there was a bit of a kerfuffle getting into his studio.

He asked if I wouldn't mind looking after the house while he was away. He told me I was welcome to stay and could take the front bedroom, the one looking out onto the lake. Use as much wood as you need when things get cold, he said, telling me that he'd stored some wood in the small shed at the back of the kitchen. As for the garden, he would arrange for someone to attend to it eventually. He looked out at the overgrown yard, staring into the middle distance for some time. Hard to believe it was so well turned out a month ago, he said. Look at it now! Look at the vines, taking over. The whole place will be swallowed up by this damn jungle one of these days... Now, make sure all doors are locked at all times, especially my studio. I wouldn't ask anyone else but you, Gary... And could you please take my car for a drive from time to time? I'm thinking of the battery, you know...

I didn't interrupt him. It was all very confusing. He was going for a trip? What trip? Whereabouts? And not a word about Lucie. He didn't mention her name, as if she'd never existed. Where is she?

We finished our coffee. After a while, without wanting to appear nosy, I asked him where he intended to go. I've been instructed to have a rest, he explained. Longland isn't good for me in my current state. I've booked a room at a Broome resort. You know, a nice relaxing place where massages are on call, where I can recline by the pool with a cocktail. I'll feel so much better there.

For whatever reason, Ernest couldn't look me in the eye. He stood up, washed our cups, dried them both and placed them in the cupboard. He then grabbed his jacket and leather hat from the coat rack and made his way to the front door. His suitcase was already packed. I followed him as he walked outside. He adjusted his hat, gazing at the forest. Several times he looked at his watch, as if waiting for the next train to arrive. They should be here any minute now, he said. I warily asked him if he'd called a taxi. I didn't get an answer. I was perplexed as to what was going on, thinking maybe Ernest had completely lost his marbles. But it all fell into place when I saw the police car come down the driveway.

He didn't say goodbye. He didn't look at me. Had it not been a police car, I might have thought he was off to the airport. One of the two policemen invited Ernest to take a seat in the back. He took his seat without protest and the policeman sat next to him. And they drove off... I felt like fainting and had to sit down. I never thought your investigation would end up like this, with Ernest taken away in a police car.

Is it too early to ask what charges have been laid against him? Yes, the sitting-room... We'd better have a seat? Really? What do you want to tell me? Surely it can't be true... Charged with assault and the attempted murder of Lucie Bruyère? My God, murder... Did he admit to it? Oh no, oh no! And with his grandfather's rifle? Those two gunshots... That was Ernest?

Oh no, not Annette! He admitted to battery and assault on Annette Serani? All those years ago? Oh, Ernest, what have you done? Officer Lawson, I can't help my tears. Ernest is like a brother to me. I've tried my best to help him in life... But really, I have failed, haven't I? I always thought Ernest could transform his rage into art...

Yes, I did hear about the second skull found in the lake. I actually heard about it when I was in Watooga this morning. I stopped there to buy cigarettes and the whole place was talking about that second skull. There was even a report on the front page of the local paper about the "macabre discovery in Longland". They say it's a child's skull, could be related to a hunting accident that goes back to 1901. The case has never been solved. According to the newspaper a mother and her eight-year-old daughter were shot dead. Am I right?

Do you mind if I ask what happened exactly? It wasn't a hunting accident but a double murder? Killed with an axe? Good God! No one was ever convicted... Are we talking about the same people who built Longland? The Germans? And do you know who killed them, the poor woman and her daughter? The father... no! The father killed them both with an axe... what a tragedy! May I ask the name of the little girl who was murdered? Sarah? On the night of the party, June Letourneau, Nicole's daughter, called out that name... Yes, she called out "Sarah" when we were outside... She said she'd seen a little girl on the lake whose name was Sarah... June is also eight-years-old, you know...

Do you remember Lucie's brooch, Lawson? The two skulls, the two heads in a shroud. Magritte's *The Lovers*, remember?

I've got to tell you, the most unusual thing happened to me when I stopped in Watooga this morning. A very strange thing... Well, a woman, in her nineties, who seemed half-blind, was seated on a fold-up chair outside the supermarket. She was selling tickets for a raffle. I could see she was talking to herself. I didn't pay much attention to her mumbling, but then I picked up on something familiar. I hadn't heard Polish since my father died twenty years ago, but I immediately recognised my native language, the only tongue we spoke at home. I stopped and bought a ticket. And I understood that her mumbling was really a prayer for the dead. Yes, she was mourning the mother and the daughter whose remains were found in the lake.

While I stood listening to the old woman, details of the party came back to me... Peculiar visions... Remember, I told you when we last met about the presences I had felt around the lake, how Lucie had been pulled away in the most unexpected way. Yes, it almost looked as if she had been forcefully dragged away... I'm sure Lucie had no intention of swimming across the lake... Of course not... It was freezing cold... But for some reason, she couldn't resist... And I remember being drawn towards the marshes myself, struggling to return to firmer ground... And when Nicole, Rosy and I were searching the caretaker's house, they too heard the voices calling from around the lake.

As I started walking back to my car, I was stopped in my tracks by the old woman's singing of the Kaddish. My eyes welled up with tears... I chanted along... *Yisgadal v'yiskadash shmay rabba... B'alma divra chirusei... v'yamlich malchusei v'yamlich malchusei...* That would translate, Officer Lawson, into something like... May His great Name grow exalted and sanctified... in the world that He created as He willed...

When she heard me, the old woman slowly lifted her face and smiled. My father taught me these prayers. I sing the Kaddish when I visit my father's grave, on the anniversary of his death... He died in springtime... The peach tree in the garden was in bloom... My parents left Poland before it was too late... I was born in Moscow... Anyway, standing there this morning, I watched people walk past, lost as I was in thought, before I got into my car and drove to Longland...

And so, your men took Ernest away. And I went back inside the house, curious to inspect Ernest's more recent paintings. That being said, I was apprehensive as to what I might find. I walked through the house... Down the long and dark corridor, the same mouldy smell... This is a terribly gloomy house. And when I pushed open the door to his studio, the shock! Everything, yes, everything had been splashed with red paint, dripping wet with it. Ernest must have emptied several drums of scarlet acrylic. His canvasses, the walls, the floor, the old books from his father's library, were soaked red... Everything there was ruined. *The Origin of the World*? Annihilated! The painting had been torn to pieces with a carving knife, still lying on the floor in a pool of red paint... I couldn't rescue a thing. Not a thing! All his paintings, wasted. I'll never know what his last works looked like...

I stepped back, locked the door, the brand-new door. I wandered around and went to the terrace. I looked out to the lake. I thought of the mother and daughter, shot dead, I should say murdered, of my grandparents and my cousins, also murdered, at Treblinka... I thought of the Dharawal people who used to live in this forest not so long ago... You've got to wonder what sort of terrible things happened when the settlers took the land and drove the Aborigines out. God only knows how much blood has been spilled around Longland... And so I started humming the Kaddish for all of them...

Yes, it dawned on me that I had an important task ahead, a work to be continued, and henceforth my duty would be to stay here, in Longland. To help the dead, to help Ernest, to wait for his return, to look after his place as I had been asked to do, try to accept him despite his illness, despite his wrong deeds, try to understand why pain prevents us from loving.

I'm not trying to make allowances for Ernest's

behaviour, Officer Lawson. What he's done is unforgivable, still, believe me, I know his entire story. I know where he comes from, and it's sinister... His father was a cruel man, a vicious monster. I've seen the scars from that time, the deep scars... There's one on his right shoulder, as though a piece of flesh had been gouged out. One day, his father tied him up to a post in the woodshed and lay into him with a length of rubber hose. Ernest was only thirteen. He was left unconscious.

His mother, well, she didn't want to know about the beatings. She kept silent when it came to shame and conflict. It didn't stop her from attending mass on Sundays... She always turned a blind eye to the old man's cruelty, rejecting her poor sod of a son, thinking he was queer but never trying to understand what he was really about. No, we didn't talk about those things, gosh, no queers in the family, for God's sake. But Ernest wasn't queer... Ernest is not a homosexual... I have shared an apartment with him for several years, I know...

I'll recount a poignant confession Ernest made to me once. One night he was very drunk... He could only open up when he was drunk... He told me that something in him had been broken. He remembered the sorts of emotions, those of joy and pleasure, he had felt before the beatings started. He remembered watching the eels in the brook, the dragonflies, the lyrebirds, drawing up an intensity of feeling from his contemplation. One day, drunkenly weeping, he told me about an occasion when he'd been most viciously hit and humiliated and his father had said to him, you poofter bastard, you're not worth cleaning the muck from my shoes. You see, he never forgot these very words. Neither did I. And from that day, when he returned to the brook and looked at the eels, the dragonflies, the lyrebirds, no emotion stirred in him. Nothing, no pleasure, no pain, no desire, nothing. He killed small animals, he said to me sobbing, and felt no sorrow. He kept at it, disturbed by what was happening to him, but his heart had hardened, dried up. His empathy for the world around him had been annihilated.

For many years he has worked at restoring that connection, the mysterious thread, because he knows that without that link, he'll never be able to move upwards, heavenwards, as he says. Ernest is a thirsty ghost looking for a spring in a desert, desperately looking, but as he gets closer, the spring turns into a mirage. Somehow Ernest has never stopped being that boy of thirteen tied to a post in the woodshed.

Yet the most astonishing and miraculous thing

is that Ernest's painting is moving, it's heart-wrenching, inspiring and poignant... I was deeply moved when I first set eyes on his work, and I'm not the only one. Many worship his art... This is a mystery...

Sometimes you stand in awe before a beautiful painting, then you discover its creator is an appalling piece of humanity. I am an art dealer... I've experienced this many times. I've come to the conclusion that there are two selves within the artist's soul that grow at different speeds: the transcendent self, brought to life through art and only visible in the work itself, and the ordinary self. The transcendent self, partially awoken and inspired, is walking ahead, while the gross self trundles along to catch up. But they don't always meet...

Yes, today was a dreadful day, but an important one... I've made the decision to close my gallery a while and wait for Ernest's return. You look surprised... Yes, well, the gallery, honestly, I'm tired of it... I'm tired of selling art to people who don't even look at what they buy. They enter my gallery, flash their Amex Platinum, only think in terms of market value and profit, and quite frankly, I've had enough, I'm fed up with it... This is not what I dreamt of when I started my career in art. Today,

I've been pondering and I now know I have better and bigger things to do.

First of all, I'll clean Ernest's studio, just like I did years ago. Our old apartment was repainted so many times. It's no big deal for me. Yes, I'm going to clean the studio before the red paint dries. That way, everything will be back in its place when Ernest returns. Because Ernest *has* to paint. If I don't help him, who else will?

Yes, today was an important day. I've made up my mind. I'm going to stay here a while. I will sleep in the front bedroom, as Ernest suggested, the one facing out onto the lake. It used to be Raphaël's bedroom… I will stay here, carry on with unfinished business and pray for the innocents, pray for the dead, pray for Ernest… And help him to find a good lawyer. Someone who'll get it right.

Jean Lucien
Faubourg Saint-Honoré
Paris
France

Gentlemen, I had a phone call yesterday evening just after seven... I was overcome... Oh... Even now, telling you about it makes my head spin... Excuse me while I take a seat. Ahem... She called me... Yes, it was yesterday, just after seven, when the phone rang. It's unusual for me to get a call so late... I wondered who it was... It was Mademoiselle Bruyère... Good heavens! She told me that she was in good health, that she'd been caught up in difficult matters... I didn't wish to pry, I had a good idea of the matters she was referring to...

Oh yes, I know... I know... Inspecteur Agnelli called me last week. That was considerate of him. He gave me an update of what had been happening in Australia... How that man, that Renfield, had aimed a rifle at Lucie... A hunting gun... The poor child must have been terrified... She managed to escape unscathed, ran through the dark forest and found her way to the road... walked several kilometres to the nearest township... Watooga, I believe, then caught the first train to Sydney and ended up roaming the city streets, destitute, for almost a month. Can you imagine, gentlemen? She had to beg to feed herself. She slept out in the open… A police patrol found her, penniless, gaunt, dirty… She was in such poor physical and emotional state they had her hospitalised immediately… Despite her ordeal, Lucie sounded joyful on the phone… Joyful and truly alive… Thank God!

Where is she now? Well, she's in a women's shelter on Sydney's North Shore. She said she was being well looked after. I was so delighted to hear that as soon as she's able, she would resume her work on the biography.

She said she would start with a chapter about Stalag VIII-A, where I was held captive. See gentlemen, I was caught by German soldiers in June 1940… on 20 June… I was then deported in a cattle truck all the way to the eastern border of Germany… to Görlitz, in Silesia, where there were thirty thousand prisoners, mostly French… There I met my friend Olivier Messiaen. But I think I've already shared some of that story with you…

Lucie was well acquainted with Messiaen's work when she and I first met, though my name was unknown to her. She was fascinated by his *Quartet for the End of Time*, and as she and I talked about my friendship with him, she grew captivated by his personality. She felt she had something in common with him.

Prisoners of war were not doomed to be exterminated… I remember life in Stalag VIII-A as if it were yesterday… In any case, Messiaen arrived in Görlitz in May '40 and between May and January '41, he wrote his famous *Quartet*… Yes… As you are a musician, the German camp commander told him, I will put you in the washhouse with a piece of bread and some manuscript paper and you will write music. Messiaen wasn't subjected to daily chores, as we were. Thus, he had time to compose… We were forbidden from disturbing him.

Still, Messiaen's life was harsh. He would not be repatriated until spring '41. We had very little to eat. A bowl of soup a day. Messiaen was so hungry that he hallucinated, saw colours and heard sounds, coloured sounds, as he put it. He saw rainbows, aurora borealis, and he turned these colours into sounds… The German camp commander will be remembered for that gesture… And the cellist Jules Malter and the clarinettist André Tanaker… prisoners at Stalag VIII-A too… When Messiaen realised he had three professional musicians, it spurred him on to write a large piece of music. As for the instruments, André and I still had our violin and clarinet. Jules was taken to Görlitz by armed guards to find a cello, something less than the sixty marks he had collected from his fellow inmates. Later we were given a worse-for-wear piano, such a bad instrument that some keys wouldn't lift back. Messiaen was the pianist, a most virtuosic one...

We gave a concert every Saturday afternoon... We drew strength from it... Our first performance of the *Quartet* was on 15 January 1941. It was freezing cold. The Stalag was buried under snow. In Silesia, the temperature can drop to minus thirty-two... We had an audience of five thousand people, all prisoners like us... priests, doctors, labourers, shopkeepers, farmers, servicemen... We could see an ocean of men, haggard, shivering from the cold... André, Jules and I, in our rags and wooden clogs. Messiaen wore a tattered bottle-green outfit that had belonged to a Czech soldier...

Most of the audience had never attended a concert in their lives and to the listener Messiaen's music can be hard work. Among the few miniature scores Messiaen had with him was Berg's *Lyric Suite*. It gave us, musicians, an idea of what he was inspired by and seeking to create... Messiaen's music is atonal... it was new for that epoch... difficult to play... To our amazement, the audience listened in devout silence.

After the performance, Messiaen said to us that never before had his music been listened to with such rapt *attention* and deep *understanding*. Yes, that's what he told us. Our fellow prisoners had been transported, overwhelmed by the beauty of Messiaen's music... music of the soul... as if all suffering had stopped... Not everyone I've met and told my story to has fully grasped why at the Stalag we turned so solemnly to music for moral and spiritual comfort... Lucie did, she understood.

Messiaen gave us much more than music during his captivity... How can I explain? He had an indefectible faith. Love, understanding, compassion, hope were his credo. He was known around the camp for his kindness... He enabled others to turn to music for solace. In this time of great destitution, he turned to what was essential to him: faith and music. Men would knock at Messiaen's door and ask for advice, comfort, encouragement... They were desperate, they missed their home, their wives, their children, their parents, they wondered if they would ever leave the camp, if they would survive... We had no idea how long the war would last, what was in store for us, whether it would be illness, a forced march, death... We didn't know. We were physical wrecks, and mentally exhausted. Messiaen was an example to us all. A source of strength. He would patiently dispense words of hope, restore fortitude, without proselytising, without pushing his Christianity down our throats. Every day, he woke up at five "to keep watch", as he said. And he did. He kept watch. Over himself. Over us.

At dawn, he listened to the birds, the angels' voices, as he called them... They found their way into his scores. Birdsongs became a new musical language. Lucie knew that Messiaen had travelled the world to record hundreds and hundreds of bird songs. Yes... Yes... With his wife Yvonne... America, New Caledonia, Australia, New Zealand... Lucie too had recorded some of the Australian birds... At dawn, she taped their songs and took photos of them... She doesn't know yet what she'll do with that material... It helps her think, she said, provides joy...

Messiaen has been an inspiration for me, for his fellow prisoners, and I believe he can still be an inspiration for us all... See, there was no anger in him. He absolutely abhorred war, hatred, wickedness. He was a true pacifist.

Lucie knows through experience that art is our most faithful friend. She plays music, did you know? She plays the piano, yes. One day, towards the end of our three weeks of interviews, as we were getting to know each other, she told me art was what she clung on to when everything around her fell apart. We, too, survived in the Stalag through art. Music, poetry, literature became our daily bread... And they accompanied us in death too. See, when our fellow prisoners were dying, those who could not find a prayer would still find a way to lessen their pain by reciting a poem. Dante, Mallarmé, Rimbaud... We whispered to our comrades the verses we could remember from school... For those who had no religion, like me, poetry was the consolation. I'm fond of Baudelaire and knew many of his poems by heart...

It's time, old Captain, left anchor, sink!
The Land rots, we shall sail into the night;
If now the sky and the sea are black as ink,
Our hearts, as you must know, are filled with light...

Ta, ta, ta! "To drown in the abyss – heaven or hell... Who cares? Through the unknown, we'll find the new." Sorry, gentlemen... I've now forgotten what follows...

Lucie confided that she would have liked to knock on Messiaen's door to find solace. She urged me to reveal as many details as I could from my time with Messiaen at the Stalag... Talk to me about his divine music! Talk to me about your Saturdays! I love the music and the man so much, Monsieur

Lucien, she often said. I will help you remember...

Well... ahem... that's what we talked about yesterday on the phone. Messiaen, again... The Saturdays... The washhouse in the snow... The birds at dawn... Then I asked her how she intended to resume her project... How would she make a living? Lucie shunned my question. I offered to send her some money, to help her through... You can always repay me later or consider it a gift, I said. She was quiet at first, then she burst into tears, accepted the money and thanked me... If I don't help her, who will?

Coming back? No, she didn't talk about coming back to France... Well, of course, I offered to accommodate her. I told her she was very welcome at my place, here in Paris or in Beaux-de-Provence, any time. But she said she'd prefer to stay in Australia. Yes, she would try to have another go over there, that's what she said... I'll try to have another go and be happy, were her words. In Australia.

ACKNOWLEDGMENTS

Thank you, merci, is too small a word to express my gratitude to the friends who have helped and supported me over the last four years. This novel would have never seen the light of day without their generous patronage. To honour our friendship I dream of another word broad enough to encompass not only friendship but also sisterhood, loyalty, complicity, esteem, care and love.

But there is no such word.

Still, I wish to thank you all from the bottom of my heart.

Thanks to Tom, my husband, who spent many hours reading the successive drafts of my manuscript before patiently editing them.

Thanks to Dominique Joly, Caroline Chatignol, Jean-Luc Chatignol, Xavier Hennekinne and Tim Herbert for being my generous and inspiring patrons.

Thanks to Jan Cornall and Karen Lane for giving me enough assurance to write my novel in a language other than mine.

Thanks to Céline Poirier who has helped me in the darkest days of my life.

Thanks to you all.

MERCI.

Love is as love does.

www.ingramcontent.com/pod-product-compliance
Lightning Source LLC
LaVergne TN
LVHW091130080826
845145LV00008B/2109

* 9 7 8 0 9 8 7 6 1 9 1 1 2 *